The Stallion and His Peculiar Boy

M.J. Evans

Dancing Horse Press Foxfield, CO

M.J. Evans/Dancing Horse Press
7013 S. Telluride St., Foxfield, CO 80016
www.dancinghorsepress.com

Publishers Cataloging-In-Publication Data
Name: M.J. Evans, Author
Title: The Stallion and His Peculiar Boy/ M.J. Evans
Description: Foxfield, Colorado: Dancing Horse Press (2021)/ Interest, Age Level: 13 and up / Includes bibliographical references. / Summary: During WWII the Nazis captured a famous Arabian stallion named Witez II from Poland and shipped him to Czechoslovakia to be part of their breeding program. An autistic boy from the village becomes his life-long groom.
Subjects: Horses – United States—History – Young Adult – Historical Fiction – Horsemen and Horsewomen – World War II – Operation Cowboy – Nazis – Autism – Horse Therapy

Ordering Information:
Quantity sales. Special discounts are available on quantity purchases by corporations, associations, and others. For details, contact the "Special Sales Department" at the address above.

The Stallion and His Peculiar Boy M.J. Evans. -- 1st ed.
ISBN 978-1-7373618-6-2

The Stallion and His Peculiar Boy

Based on the Life of the Famous Arabian Horse Witez II

Contents

PART 1

NAZI CAPTIVE

As the misty dawn broke over the meadows at Janow, Poland on April 1, 1938, a beautiful Arabian mare named Federacja foaled a bay colt by Ofir. The eagerly anticipated colt was one of fifteen due in 1938 sired by the brightest star in the Polish directory of Arabian stallions.

The Poles had been breeding Arabians since the sixteenth century, and Ofir had been the product of a dessert-bred stallion brought to Poland to continue the improvement of the breed. Now, a new colt would carry on the line and prove the rule: "Breed the best to the best, and you can't go wrong."

He was given the name Witez II, but called simply Witez (pronounced VEE-tez,) meaning chieftain and knight, prince and hero, all rolled into one.

But a dark cloud was looming on the horizon, a cloud that would change the life of Witez forever.

Chapter 1

Hostau, Czechoslovakia, September 1943

The man's fist came down on the table with a bang that shook the dishes and rattled the silverware. "Look at me when I speak to you, boy!" The father, large and muscular, glared across the table at his son.

An eleven-year-old lad with curly brown hair continued to stare down at his hands with his large brown eyes. His fingers fiddled with the napkin in his lap. His upper body started rocking—forward and back, forward and back.

Turning to his wife, the man spoke through clenched teeth. "Get him out of my sight."

The small, frail woman pushed her chair back and stood. Her plain facial features hid the fear she kept bottled inside. She hurried to the end of the table and placed a hand gently on the boy's shoulder. "Teodor, come with me." Looking at her son, her features softened. The boy was thin, and small for his age, and her heart went out to him as he displayed obvious distress, his facial features contorting, his rocking continuing.

She slid her hand down his arm and lifted him by the elbow. As Teodor stood, his napkin fell to the floor. He let out a guttural groan, jerked away from his mother, and bent down to pick it up. Carefully, he folded the cloth and placed it next to his plate, lining up the bottom edge with that of the table.

Back in his room, Teodor sat upon the window seat and lined up his colored blocks in a perfect pattern . . . red, black, yellow, green, red, black, yellow, green . . . along the windowsill.

He listened as his father's harsh Czech rant wafted up the narrow staircase.

"I swear, you must be the worst mother in the world to have raised such an insolent, ignorant, and stupid boy," the man said with a snarl. "Why, he doesn't even talk. He just grunts like a pig."

The woman, her body bent over, the tears burning the backs of her eyes, struggled with her whispered response. "Teodor isn't stupid, and I have done my best to be a good mother."

"Well, it hasn't been good enough," the man snapped as he rose from his chair and stomped around the table. Stopping in front of her, he added, "Then, you tell me what's the matter with him." He pressed his abnormally large fists into his sides.

The woman dropped her chin and shook her head. "I don't know. But I know he isn't stupid . . . he's just . . . peculiar."

"Peculiar!" the man shouted. "That's a good one. Ha! He's so peculiar, the school won't let him attend."

"They just don't understand him."

"And you do?"

"No. But I'm willing to try to help him."

The man sneered. "And how have you helped him? He won't talk even when spoken to. He won't look me in the eye. I've tried to be a good husband and father, but I'm at my wit's end. I can't take any more of this, Agata."

Startled, the woman looked up. The darkness in her husband's face frightened her. "What are you saying?'

"I am going to join the resistance fighters."

"You're going to leave Czechoslovakia?"

"Where have you been, stupid woman? Czechoslovakia has ceased to exist since the Nazis invaded us in March of 1939. I am going to fight to get it back."

A moan of anguish rose from deep within her soul as she collapsed to the ground, grasping her husband around his knees. "Oh, husband, I fear if you do this, we will never see you again. I have heard terrible stories about the fate of the resistance fighters."

Unmoved by her tears, the man folded his arms across his chest. "Well, I can't stand idly by as our country is destroyed."

"But all is well in Hostau. The Nazis here have not caused us any trouble. We are protected by the mountains and thick forests that surround us. We're too far away from the fighting."

"Have you not seen what is going on at the Stud? The Nazis are shipping in hundreds of horses."

"But very few soldiers."

"For now. But I'm not foolish enough to think that will last. I'm going to join the resistance, and that is the end of it." He pulled away from her. "I will be leaving in the morning."

The sun was just coming over the eastern forest, causing shadows to move up the main street of the little village of Hostau. Located fifteen miles from the southeastern Bavarian border and separated from the capital of

Prague by hundreds of miles of forest and mountains, Hostau was home to a little more than one thousand residents. The pretty, German-style Tudor houses stood proudly side by side along the steep, narrow street leading up to the small plaza. Beside the plaza stood St. Jakobus Church with its yellow plaster sides and red-tiled roof. Perched proudly on top was its pointed steeple. The church was the home to the Catholic parish which had been established in 1384. It provided the spiritual home for the faithful in Hostau and the care of the cemetery at the southern end of town.

Just beyond the church was a handsome castle, once the home of the Prince of Trauttmansdorff but now the German Army's headquarters. Most of the members of the army unit were sent there to work the horse breeding operation at the Hostau Stud. The castle looked more like a French château than a fortress. It was built in an "L" shape and painted white. The building bordered the formal courtyard and gardens.

Opposite the castle was the Stud. A horse breeding farm, the Stud was founded in 1914. During World War I, the facility was expropriated by the state and converted to a military stud farm. When the Nazis invaded

Czechoslovakia in 1939, the German Army took over the Stud. In 1942, Hitler's forces began moving hundreds of broodmares and select stallions to the Hostau Stud. Mechanization had not yet fully replaced the horse in the German army. The finest horses had been taken from their homes all over western Europe: Austria, Yugoslavia, Italy, and Poland, to name a few. Hitler appointed Gustav Rau with the task of overseeing all the Studs in German-occupied lands. The well-known horseman was responsible for providing the army with the 6,000 fresh horses it needed every month to keep the war effort going. Rau was also charged with using what knowledge of horse husbandry was available at the time to breed the perfect warhorse.

Teodor sat on the window seat in front of the wavy-glassed windowpanes kept clean by his devoted mother. He watched the people on the street below emerge from their houses that lined the all-too-familiar narrow road. He had been born in this house, as had his mother, his grandfather, and his great-grandfather. His family carried with them a great deal of pride at being what they called "True Czechs" as opposed to the "Sudeten-Germans."

From his perch, Teodor watched the tiny world go by, a world into which he had been born but had experienced very little. He neither desired, nor was given the opportunity, to interact with it. He left his home only on the rare occasion that his mother took him to Mass or to the village shops. Taking him away from the comfort of his room usually resulted in temper tantrums, though these had become fewer and farther between as he had gotten older. Still, his father and mother were shamed by his behavior and preferred to just keep him at home. While his father lacked the ability to offer him any affection, his mother doubled her efforts to smother him with both love and patience. Each day she strove to teach him his numbers and letters while trying to find a way inside his mind. Teodor offered her little reward for her efforts.

On this day, as he was staring out the window, he saw his father step out of their house and onto the stoop. The man was dressed in a warm wool overcoat and his favorite black fedora with a silver pin attached to the felt brim. In his left hand, he clutched a weathered, leather satchel. He paused before stepping onto the main street. Turning, he looked up at Teodor's window. He took his hat from his head, removed the silver pin bearing the family crest, lifted it toward Teodor's window then bent down and set it on the top step. He replaced his hat and offered his son a brief salute by touching the brim. Teodor did not acknowledge his father's gesture, neither through eye contact nor facial response. His father shrugged his shoulders, turned, and walked toward the cemetery, leaving the pin to sparkle in the new morning sun.

Chapter 2

Janów Podlaski, Poland, May 1944

The beautiful stud farm located in Janów Podlaski, established in 1817, was the oldest state stud farm in Poland and also the most elegant. Its clock tower stood proudly over the tidy and well-cared-for barns in a classic, Old-World way.

Home to the beloved Polish Arabians, the farm was located just a few miles from the Soviet border, site of many of the ferocious and deadly battles between the Red Army and the Nazis in this years-long war. This put the horses in a dangerous position. Rau feared for their safety, especially the ones he wanted for his breeding program. So, in early May of 1944, he sent orders to the Stud to have nine of the most magnificent stallions sent by train to Hostau, Czechoslovakia. Overseeing all the breeding farms now under German control, Rau designated the Hostau Stud as the site for his experiments in line breeding. Line breeding was the practice of breeding father to daughter or other close relatives, intending to pass along and accentuate the finest qualities in both.

One of the horses he selected to be moved away from Poland was a beautiful, fifteen-hand Bay named Witez II. Witez was the most valuable of all the stallions, being a son of the famous stud, Ofir. The horse was a true gentleman, unlike many of his companions. As he was led to the ramp leading into the dark train car that would carry him away from the only home he had ever known, Witez did little more than prick his ears, arch his shapely neck, and obediently follow his groom up the wooden ramp and into the stall that had been prepared for the journey.

The horses traveled for nine days – almost 600 miles. It is unlikely that they appreciated the sights as they traveled through Warsaw, Lodz, and south toward Prague. They were tired and irritable when they finally reached Hostau.

There, they were greeted by the stud master, Lieutenant Colonel Hubert Rudofsky, and a young veterinarian by the name of Rudolf Lessing. Both men were horse lovers and very knowledgeable about horse care. The stallions were soon bedded down comfortably in the stallion barn with fresh water and plenty of good quality hay.

The nine stallions had not been moved any too soon. A few days after their departure, a German bomb dropped on the farm at Janów, partially destroying one of the stallion barns. Fortunately, the stallions who remained at the Stud were out to pasture at the time.

The horsemen in Janów feared greatly for the safety of their beloved horses. Their beautiful Arabians, the pride of Poland, had been developed over the span of hundreds of years. Now, all their careful work was in danger of being destroyed. As the Soviet Army advanced, it either stole the horses it came upon, or killed and ate them.

By late June, all the horses yet remaining in Janów were evacuated to a farm in a small German town several hundred miles to the west. While their living conditions were not as luxurious as those in Janów, they were, at least for the time being, in a safer place.

But the Polish people feared they might never see their beloved Arabians again.

Chapter 3

Hostau Stud, late May 1944

Teodor and his mother never saw father and husband again. Word spread around the village of Hostau that the resistance fighters split into two groups: those who supported communism and Stalin, and those who supported the exiled democratic government led by Edvard Benes. Regardless of their loyalties, those rebels who were caught faced an unpleasant result . . . the lucky ones were killed.

Teodor and his mother suffered the scarcity brought on by war just like everyone in Hostau. Bartering for needed goods and services became commonplace. The boy's mother began taking in laundry and mending to secure the things they needed. Still, it was hard to make ends meet. Hostau had been famous for its fine linen woven fabric, its delicious honey, and its beautiful pottery. None of that seemed to be desirable anymore.

One day, while in the village square, Teodor's mother heard two men, one a German soldier, the other the town blacksmith, discussing the situation at the Stud. Many people in Hostau still clung to the old ways and spoke in Czech. These two men, however, were conversing in German. Agata was fluent in both languages, having grown up around both the native Czechs and the long-time German settlers.

"I don't know how we can keep up with all the horses the Nazi leadership is sending to us," said the soldier.

"I heard word that Gustav Rau is seeking the finest Lipizzaners, Thoroughbreds, and Arabians to develop the perfect horse," replied the blacksmith.

"Yes, that seems to be the intent. Even though the Western allies are using more machines and vehicles to fight the war, the Fuhrer is still relying on horses, almost solely, for field transport. I have been told by people close to Rau that we need over a million horses at any time just to move our weapons and supplies, not to mention those needed by the Cavalry divisions. We're having a hard time keeping up with the demand. Sadly, we are sending horses that are far too young into the battle. They get broken down pretty quickly."

"From what I have seen, the horses coming in are quite magnificent," said the blacksmith, rubbing his hands together in anticipation of work to come.

"That is true. But each horse requires a great deal of care. They aren't your typical plow horse. The horses Rau is sending us are high-spirited purebreds," the soldier said as he removed his cap and ran his fingers through his hair. Replacing the cap on his head, he added, "We just had a new batch of Arabians come in from Poland on the train. I really need help with them."

Teodor's mother gathered up the bundles of laundry she was collecting and hurried back down the hill to her house. As she worked her way home, an idea was forming in her head.

"Teodor, Mother is home," she said, dropping the laundry on the kitchen table. So as not to surprise him, for she knew surprises were difficult for Teodor, she continued talking as she climbed the stairs. "I have time to go for a walk. Would you like to come?" She reached the landing at the top of the stairs and walked to Teodor's closed door. She rapped softly on the aged wood before twisting the knob and pushing the door open.

Teodor sat just where she expected him to be . . . on the window seat, arranging and rearranging his colored blocks . . . red, black, yellow, green, red, black, yellow, green.

The mother sat beside him and stroked his curly hair. "There are some beautiful horses in the pastures. Would you like to see them?"

The boy lifted his chin and looked past his mother, as though peering into another world . . . a world that only he could see. Without speaking or looking at her, the boy stood, grasped his father's silver pin and, with it clutched tightly in his palm, walked to the door. Her heart beating rapidly, Agata followed him.

Teodor and his mother walked up the street, side by side. She was careful not to rub against him. When they reached the town's plaza, they turned toward the castle and its expansive fields now dotted with horses of all colors. In one pasture were white mares with black foals at their sides. Another field housed frolicking chestnut fillies and colts and their copper-colored or brown mothers. Teodor stopped at each field, climbed up on the bottom rail of the fence, and stared at the beautiful animals as they grazed, rolled in the waving grasses and wildflowers, or stood, heads down, sleeping in the warm spring sunshine. Each stop to watch the horses lasted many minutes, but his mother knew better than to rush him.

Beyond the fields of mares were the smaller paddocks, each holding one stallion. Once again, Teodor stopped and watched each magnificent animal. But it was at the final paddock that everything changed.

In the paddock closest to the stables, a bay Arabian stallion was trotting around the fence line, his muscles rippling with each stride. He had large, intelligent eyes and a small, delicate muzzle. His brown coat glistened in the sun. His black mane and tail flowed in the breeze.

Teodor climbed on the fence. Seeing him, the stallion stopped, turned toward the boy, and let out a loud snort. Teodor stared directly at the horse, focusing on him in a manner his mother had never seen before. Agata gasped as she watched her son extend his hand and smile.

Slowly the horse walked toward Teodor, stopping right in front of him. The mother bit her lip and waited. The boy held his position and waited. One more step and the soft dainty muzzle was in Teodor's hand.

Teodor looked into the depths of the horse's liquid, brown eyes. A link of understanding passed between them that surpassed mere affection. An assortment of intensely strong emotions washed over the boy. It was as if this horse was a long-lost friend, or someone he had been waiting to meet his entire life. His gaze remained locked on the eyes of the horse. This is where he belonged.

"Teodor's horse," the boy whispered.

Chapter 4

Hostau Stud, the same afternoon

Hearing the sound of her son's voice for the first time, speaking actual words instead of letting out screams or grunts, was enough to send the mother to her knees in tears. Words! Teodor, her son, now twelve years old, actually said his first words! It was too much to be believed. With tears streaming down her cheeks, she looked up at the horse now nuzzling her son's curly hair. This horse was a miracle-worker in her eyes, and no one would ever convince her otherwise.

From the dark recesses of the stable, a handsome young man with blond hair combed back from his forehead observed the entire encounter of boy and horse. Being a husband and father himself, his curiosity was piqued by the woman's response. At the same time, he was pleased at what he saw with the horse's reaction to the lad. He stepped out of the stable and walked purposefully toward them.

Seeing the officer approach, the woman sucked in her breath and quickly stood, brushing away the tears on her face. She smoothed out her well-worn house dress. "Hello, kind sir. I hope we are not intruding. I merely wanted my son to see the beautiful horses."

"Oh, do not worry yourself. You have done nothing wrong," he said with a smile and a slight bow of his head. His eyes twinkled, and his face radiated warmth and kindness. The man was dressed in the customary German army uniform: tan cotton twill pants tucked into tall black riding boots. His tunic was olive green, also cotton twill, with a single row of buttons down the front and pleated, flapped pockets sewn on his chest. The woman had been commissioned to repair many such shirts in the last year.

The man extended his hand. "I am Dr. Rudolf Lessing, the veterinarian here at the Stud and aide to Herr Rau."

The woman hesitated, then took his hand. "It is my pleasure to make your acquaintance. I am Agata from the village. And this is my son, Teodor."

"Ah, Agata, meaning 'Good Hearted," and Teodor, 'God's Present.' Lovely names," said the vet.

Turning to the horse he said, "Let me introduce you to Witez the Second." The vet pronounced his name as VEE-tez. He reached over and stroked the stallion's arched neck. "His name means Chieftain. He is the son of Ofir, one of the most famous Arabians ever produced by the Poles. When God created him, He broke the mold and threw it away." Eyeing the beautiful stallion with a look of adoration and a bit of respect, he added, "I have a sense that this stallion, born in 1938, is destined for greatness."

Teodor continued to look into the eyes of the horse. In one hand he clasped his father's silver pin while his other hand stroked the star centered on Witez's perfect head.

"Teodor's horse," he repeated.

Dr. Lessing let out a burst of laughter. "Don't we all wish he were ours. But this horse belongs to the Fatherland."

Gathering all the courage she could muster, Agata stepped forward. "Sir, it is my understanding that you are in need of help with the horses. As you can see, my son is a strong healthy boy. Might he be of service to you?" the mother asked, rubbing her sweating hands on her skirt.

Rudolf Lessing paused, appearing to consider the proposal. Turning to the woman, he said, "I can see that the horse is attracted to your son. If it would be pleasing to you, I need a groom for this horse. Perhaps Teodor would like to take on that responsibility. I can't pay him, but I can feed him well."

And with that, it was arranged. Teodor became groom and constant companion to Witez.

Chapter 5

The Stud, later that day

"Come with me lad," Rudolf Lessing said. "I will show you around the stable."

Agata prepared herself for an emotional outburst of resistance from Teodor. To her surprise, it didn't come. Instead, her son dropped his hand from Witez's face, turned, and followed the kindly vet. Agata stood as though frozen in place, her mouth agape, and watched him go. As the man and her son entered the darkened doors of the stable, she turned back to the horse. "I don't understand what just happened between the two of you, but thank you," she said with tears welling up in her eyes.

Perhaps it is safe to say that Teodor didn't understand what had happened either. But the moment he saw the stallion looking at him from across the field, a door opened within his mind, and he willingly stepped through it.

Until that day, neither Teodor nor his mother knew the talent that the boy had for working with horses . . . especially a special horse like Witez. And, like the rest of the world, neither Agata nor Teodor understood the mystery that would later be called autism.

Teodor followed Lessing into the darkened aisleway that went down the middle of the stable. Stalls with wooden half-walls and metal piping above them lined both sides of the structure. The smell of hay mingled with clean leather filled Teodor's lungs, and he realized instantly it was a smell he would always love. At this time of day, the horses were all at turnout, so the barn was silent except for the sound of Lessing's riding boots tapping rhythmically on the brick surface of the aisle as he marched past stall after stall

The vet stopped in front of a stall near the end of the row. "This is Witez's stall. It will be your job to make sure it is always kept free of manure and wet straw." Sliding open the door that hung from a metal track across the top of the stall's walls, Lessing went inside. "Come in, young man," he said, smiling.

Teodor had never been the recipient of a smile from a man. He cast his eyes down but obediently stepped into the stall.

Motioning around the stall, the vet gave him instructions on basic horse care. "He must always have plenty of clean water. Horses drink an amazing amount of water . . . as you will soon learn," Lessing chuckled. "You will also notice a chunk of salt for him to lick. This bucket is for his grain, which he receives twice a day. This rack is for his hay."

Teodor said nothing but his eyes followed the man around the stall as he memorized every instruction.

Leaving the stall, Lessing showed Teodor where Witez's halter and lead rope hung. "You will use this to gather him from the paddock." The man gave him a quick lesson on how to place it correctly on the horse's head. "As you lead him, insist that he stay by your right shoulder. Witez is quite the gentleman, but we don't want him to develop any bad habits."

The tour of the stable included the feed room where Teodor was shown the proper amount of grain and hay to give Witez. Next, they went to the tack room. "This is Witez's saddle and bridle. Witez will need regular exercise. Have you ever ridden a horse?

Teodor, his eyes downcast, shook his head.

"That will not be a problem," Lessing said, giving Teodor a pat on the shoulder. "I will instruct you. But perhaps we will start on one of the old mares,"

Teodor's life soon became one of a happy routine. He slept on a cot at the old farmhouse that housed the other men who worked with the horses. Most of them were German members of the military – men, not boys like Teodor, who was just approaching his teenage years. Some were prisoners of war speaking languages Teodor did not understand. Others were local men recruited to help care for the horses. The war was rarely a topic of conversation. Teodor didn't take part but listened intently to those speaking German or Czech.   These men knew so much about horses; they were able to feed Teodor's yearning for knowledge. The men were horsemen whose only concern, like that of Rudolf Lessing, was the care of the horses. The political maneuvering by military leaders was not something that concerned them. And, perhaps most importantly for the boy, no one seemed to care that Teodor seemed a bit peculiar. Their only concern was that he fulfill his share of the work.

Everyone rose early to feed the horses to which they were assigned. They cleaned the stalls and gave their horses a thorough grooming. One German soldier kindly instructed Teodor on how to properly use a curry comb, a body brush, and a hoof pick. The grooming time became a favorite for both boy and horse. Teodor found himself humming as he curried Witez's brown coat in a circular pattern. Then he brushed it until it glistened. He cleaned the stallion's hooves in the same order each day: front near, hind near, front off, hind off. Once completed, Teodor lined up his grooming tools in a neat row in the grooming box, placed in the order of use. The repetition and routine at the Stud were perfect for a peculiar boy such as Teodor.

Teodor's riding lessons began the next week. Lessing taught him how to properly tack up the old Thoroughbred mare. Again, order and routine were perfect for both boy and horse. He was shown how to lead the horse to the outdoor arena and up to the mounting block. "Stand and face the horse's saddle," Dr. Lessing instructed. "Now place your left foot in the stirrup, shift your weight onto that foot and swing your right leg over the horse's back. Sit gently down in the saddle."

Having done as instructed, Teodor found himself straddling the horse's back. Being several feet above the ground did not bother him in the least. He looked forward between the mare's ears and watched them twitch back and forth. He bent down, an arm on each side of the chestnut-colored neck and rested his cheek against her mane. He breathed in deeply the sweet smell of horse and offered one of the few smiles of his life to that point. It would not be the last. On the back of a horse, Teodor was filled with a deep sense of belonging.

For several mornings in a row, Rudolf Lessing followed the same routine for Teodor's lessons. Groom. Tack up. Mount up. Walk, halt, walk, circle. It was a bright morning, where the sunlight sparkled on the dew-covered grasses, when Lessing changed the routine. Teodor completed all the walking exercises but was surprised when Lessing called out to him. "Pick up the trot." Teodor dropped his chin and felt a quiver course through his body. "Just give her a little squeeze with your calves. You'll be fine."

Teodor whispered to the mare. "Can you trot for me?"

The mare's ears twitched forward and back, and she licked and chewed on her bit before giving a slight toss of her head.

Teodor took a deep breath. "Here goes," he whispered while giving the mare a pat on the neck. He squeezed his calves as instructed and the mare picked up a slow, smooth trot. Teodor sat up in the saddle and let his body move with the motion of the horse's long strides.

"That's it," shouted Lessing. "You've got it. You're a natural horseman."

A smile spread across Teodor's face as he lifted his eyes and looked ahead. His brown curls bounced across his forehead. The rhythmic movement of the horse's two-beat trot seemed to resonate throughout his body, and he began humming a two-beat rhythm in concert with her moving legs. He knew in his heart this was where he needed to be. This was where he would find the healing necessary to grow and develop into the young man he was capable of becoming.

Chapter 6

D-Day: June 6, 1944

All over Europe, towns lay in ruins, homes and gardens were abandoned, fields went unplanted. People whose homes had been destroyed were searching for places to sleep in peace. And still, the war stormed across the land.

The Allied forces fighting the advance of the Nazis had been given a tremendous boost when the United States, in response to the Japanese attack on Pearl Harbor in the U.S. Territory of Hawaii on December 7th, 1941, actively joined the war effort by supplying troops. During 1942, 3.9 million Americans were enlisted in the armed services. At the end of 1943, that number ballooned to 9.1 million.

By May 1944, the number of Allied troops in England was expanding by the thousands each and every day. England became a sort of staging area where millions of troops gathered to be given their supplies and orders. According to General Dwight D. Eisenhower, the entire United Kingdom had become a massive military base.

General George Patton led the Third Army, and beneath him, Colonel Hank Reed oversaw the 2nd Cavalry group. Both were horsemen of great esteem. General Patton, known for his mastery of tank combat in this war, had represented the U.S. in the 1912 Olympic Games in Stockholm. Coincidentally, both men were enthusiastic polo players and show jumpers.

On June 6, 1944, the largest amphibious invasion to ever be undertaken—Operation Overlord—took place along the French coastline at Normandy. Labeled "D-Day," more than a million troops from the United States, the United Kingdom, Canada, Poland, and France stormed the beaches and laid the foundation for the Allied defeat of Germany.

Yet, in little Hostau, the spring flowers were blooming and the blossoms on the apple trees were fluttering to the ground. The famous Hostau honeybees were busy gathering their nectar. And at the Stud, the mares with foals by their sides were grazing on the new spring grasses.

Chapter 7

Hostau Stud, Summer 1944

Teodor began exercising Witez in mid-summer. Sitting atop the stallion made the world come alive for the peculiar boy. Arena work followed a prescribed pattern set forth by Lessing and his boss, Gustav Rau. Checking on the breeding program with frequent visits, the pedagogue elicited fear among all the riders and grooms with his strict and demanding ways. No one dared to question his methods, even as several whispered behind his back that the line-breeding was resulting in several unusual birth defects in many of the foals, including misshapen hooves that resembled goats' feet.

On one such visit to the Stud, Rau stopped his walking tour of the pastures to watch the horses working in the arena. He caught sight of Teodor riding Witez. His eyes followed the boy as he took the prize stallion through the set of exercises designed to strengthen every part of the horse's body. Rau knew the quality of this stallion, the classic head, the rippling muscles beneath a gleaming brown coat. There were none like him.

"Who is that groom?" Rau asked Lessing, who was accompanying him on his tour.

"It is a boy from the village who has been assigned to Witez."

"Hmmm. Talented rider."

"Yes, Herr Rau. He is."

"Bring him over."

Lessing paused, remembering the awkward day he had introduced Teodor to Lieutenant Colonel Hubert Rudofsky, the man Herr Rau had put in charge of managing the Stud.

Rudofsky was born and raised in the old kingdom of Bohemia, a narrow strip of land populated by Germans that the Nazis called Sudetenland and considered part of Germany. Rudofsky had served Czechoslovakia before 1938, and after that had done his duty for the German Army that now controlled his home. The row of metal ribbons over his left breast pocket testified of his years of service to two nations. He was no Nazi. He was a horseman and a preeminent horse-breeding expert.

When he first encountered Teodor, the tall, bald, bespectacled Rudofsky was making his daily rounds of inspecting each horse and taking notes on everything from their condition to their diet. Rudofsky was a true lover of horses. He even refused to learn to drive a car, preferring transportation by horse or horse-drawn carriage. As he walked from barn to barn, he carried a silver-topped leather driving whip.

On Teodor's second day at the Stud, Rudofsky came upon the boy grooming Witez in his stall.

"Hello, young man," Rudofsky had said.

Teodor did not answer, nor did he look at the man in acknowledgment.

"It is customary to respond, when spoken to," Rudofsky said with a stern clip to each word.

Rudolf Lessing chanced to be nearby and hurried over. "Lieutenant Colonel Rudofsky, let me introduce you to Witez's new groom, Teodor. He is a boy from the village who seems to have an incredible connection to the horse. However, it's people he has a little trouble with."

Rudofsky smiled. "I can understand that. Given the choice between a man and a horse, I'll take a horse every time," he said with a chuckle.

Now, Lessing was faced with introducing the boy to Hitler's man in charge of developing the perfect warhorse for the Nazis. He felt his heart start to pound in his chest and his hands get clammy. "Teodor, bring Witez over here," called Lessing to the boy.

Teodor brought Witez down from a trot to an easy walk with just his seat and upper leg. He lengthened his reins and let the horse stretch his neck as they approached the fence bordering the arena.

"Teodor," Lessing said, "this is Herr Rau. He is in charge of all the German horse breeding studs. He would like to speak to you."

Teodor avoided looking directly at the older, but physically fit, man dressed in the gray German army uniform typically worn by officers. His fingers twisted Witez's black mane. "Nice to meet you," he managed to mumble.

"Young man, I am impressed with the way you ride Witez. He is one of the most valuable horses we own. An outstanding example of the Arabian breed, though I am surprised that such a fine horse could come out of such a backward country as Poland." The man snorted in disgust, as though the mention of the word "Poland" was distasteful to him. "Please make sure you are careful with him and follow Dr. Lessing's every instruction. You must keep him strong and healthy."

Teodor, his eyes still downcast, merely nodded.

As Herr Rau walked away with Dr. Lessing, Teodor heard him say, "Peculiar boy."

"Yes, but bright and talented," Lessing replied.

"I like a man of few words. They listen better," Rau said with a chuckle as he gave the vet a hard clap on the back.

Chapter 8

Hostau Stud, Autumn 1944

The best days were those when Teodor was allowed to take Witez on the path that wound through the lush forest bordering the breeding farm to the west. The thick growth of trees covering the low but ragged mountainous area called the Bohemian Forest was not just a beautiful backdrop for the farm but also formed a barrier between Germany and Austria that had withstood invasion for centuries. The Czech's luck changed as Hitler and his army moved throughout Europe, and Austria succumbed to promises of wealth and security. This left Czechoslovakia, which was made an independent country after World War I, an easy target.

On the back of his horse, however, none of this mattered to Teodor. Here he could experience the world in a way he had never before been able to do. He lifted his eyes beyond Witez's ears and looked up into the thick canopy of branches from the triangularly shaped linden trees as they reached over his head. He listened to the chattering of the squirrels as they scolded him for entering their domain. He breathed deeply of the forest smells intensified by the summer heat. Dappled light and shade danced across the pathways.

The rhythmic four-beat walk of the horse beneath him made him feel alive. Memories of his childhood flashed through his brain. In his mind's eye he saw himself as a little boy throwing a temper tantrum . . . at what, he did not remember, nor did it matter. It could have been the loss of a toy, a meal that he didn't like, someone moving a shoe he had placed intentionally in a special spot . . . anything that disrupted the order of things. The only thing that could get him to stop screaming and pounding his head with his fists was a walk in the forest. His wise mother grabbed his hand and pulled him to the backyard and into the forest. The moment his feet touched the leaf and twig-covered ground, his tantrum evaporated like snow on a warm, sunny day. His father accused his mother of being overly indulgent. But it always worked, and anything she found that controlled Teodor, or helped him control himself, she continued to do.

On Witez's back, riding through the forest, the war and bloodshed all over Europe seemed far, far away, and the world seemed to be in proper order.

At times, Dr. Lessing joined Teodor on his rides through the forest. He always rode his favorite horse, Indigo.

"Teodor, I want you to know that I am pleased with the care you are giving Witez. His stall is always clean. His water is sparkling. His manger is filled with sweet, fresh hay. His tack and grooming supplies are always left clean and orderly. You even keep the aisleway in front of his stall swept."

Teodor, his eyes looking straight ahead, offered a brief smile. "Teodor loves Witez," was all he said.

Teodor often returned home to partake of the evening meal with his mother. Agata was both amazed and pleased by the progress her son was making while working at the Stud. "When you come from the Stud, you are smiling, and your eyes are sparkling. That makes me think you feel happy. Are you happy, Teodor?' she asked.

Staring down at his food, he swallowed his bite of potatoes. He breathed in the eternal smell of baking bread and boiled onions coming from the kitchen. "Yes," he finally said, his voice little more than a whisper.

"What makes you happy?"

"Witez."

"I came to watch you ride, yesterday. Did you see me?"

Teodor shook his head, still not looking up at his mother.

"You ride beautifully."

Teodor nodded. "Teodor loves Witez."

One November day in the late fall of 1944, as Teodor was in Witez's stall, giving his tail a brushing, he heard the gruff voice of Gustav Rau over the clipping sound of two sets of boots on the brick floor of the aisleway.

"The Soviet Army has withstood the advances by the Fatherland and is now moving west. I was just informed that the Red Army has captured the horses at the Royal Hungarian Riding School."

The sound of the footsteps stopped.

"I am shocked and sorry to hear that."

Teodor recognized the voice of Rudofsky.

"What has become of the horses?" Rudofsky asked.

Teodor leaned toward the door to hear the answer.

"We do not know for sure, but it doesn't sound good. The Russian Army is starving. I doubt they would care if they were eating an old plow horse or a champion Lipizzaner."

Suddenly, the war seemed very real and very dangerous. Teodor threw his arms around Witez's neck as a tear coursed down his cheek. "Teodor will never let anyone hurt you," he whispered in the stallion's ear.

Chapter 9

The heavy winter snow blew into drifts against the north sides of the whitewashed stone barns of Hostau Stud. Built in a U formation around a large, central courtyard, the Stud had been expanded over the years so that there were now separate barns for the mares and foals, the stallions, and the horses in training. A large, enclosed arena was attached to the training barn. To one side of the stallion barn was a large outdoor arena, currently covered in snow and not in use. The bare branches of the large linden trees that lined the drive testified to the harshness of the Czechoslovakian winters. The gray sky melted into the similarly colored slate roofs which melted into the ice-covered gravel of the courtyard. Bleak would best describe the Stud in the dead of winter.

Inside the barns, however, the work didn't slow down with the arrival of winter. In fact, the bitter weather added more tasks to the always long list. As Lessing had said, horses indeed drank a lot of water, and ice continually formed on the surface of the tanks and buckets. Teodor broke up the ice in Witez's bucket several times a day. He kept the stallion's stall clean, and the straw fluffed up. Since Lessing didn't want to take a chance with horses getting injured in the slick snow, Teodor spent several hours each day hand-walking the stallion up and down the aisles inside the barn.

Teodor kept his eyes on the ground as he walked, rarely speaking to the other grooms. They were all accustomed to the peculiar boy by now and no one seemed to mind. Indeed, they admired the bond Witez had with the boy. For the last six months, the two had been inseparable.

As the young teen and his horse walked up and down, back and forth between the stalls, Witez nudged Teodor's shoulder and rubbed his cheek against the boy. "Good boy," Teodor whispered. His heart swelled with joy, and he stopped to give Witez a rub on the neck.

Due to the large number of horses at the Stud, time for riding in the covered arena was limited. But Teodor relished the time he was able to be in the saddle. While he couldn't put into words what Witez had done for him, and continued to do for him, he knew he had been changed.

While the scourge of evil continued to spread death and destruction across Europe, the Stud at little Hostau was experiencing a season of new life. Winter meant the stable was on high alert as foaling season arrived and mares went into labor. One bitterly cold and snowy February day, Teodor was just dismounting Witez after their short workout in the arena when Dr. Lessing rushed up to him. "Teodor, I need your help. We have seven mares in labor. I need you to keep an eye on Amara."

A brief look of fear fluttered across Teodor's face.

"Don't worry," said the vet, picking up on Teodor's concern, "I just need you to watch to make sure all is well. I'll be close at hand. You can call me if needed."

Teodor quickly removed Witez's tack, gave him a brief rubdown, and put on his stable blanket. Finally, he made sure the horse had some hay and water.

The mare barn was across the courtyard from the stable that housed the stallions.

Teodor rushed out the barn door and was immediately greeted with a blast of cold air and swirling snowflakes. He buttoned his jacket and lifted the collar for protection as he hurried across the courtyard to the lovely mare barn. The structure was built solidly with old stones and a slate roof. The boy entered, stepping onto the brick-paved aisleway. The familiar and welcome smell of horseflesh filled the place. He paused to let his eyes adjust to the dim light before walking forward in search of the vet.

Lessing was in a stall with one of the mares when Teodor entered the barn.

"Dr. Lessing," Teodor said, looking down at his hands as they twisted his shirt tails.

"Oh, Teodor," the vet said. "I'm glad you're here. Thank you for coming so quickly. Amara started waxing yesterday. That is when the teats start emitting a thick yellowish substance. That generally happens six to forty-eight hours before labor starts."

Teodor nodded his head and stared at the mare where she stood in the center of her stall. Her eyelids were half-closed, and her head was drooping to the level of her knees.

"I want you to stay in the corner of the stall," Lessing said, placing a gentle hand on Teodor's shoulder. "Do not bother her. But don't leave unless she seems to be having trouble. If it seems things are not going well, come find me. I'll be checking on all the mares in labor." Lessing stepped toward the stall door. Turning back, he added, "It might be a long night, young man, so make yourself comfortable."

Teodor nodded again, then walked across the large box stall and let his back slide down the stone wall until he was nestled in the deep straw. Amara shuffled through the straw to where he was sitting and dropped her head in his lap.

The boy rubbed her forehead and stroked her ears. He noticed her rhythmic breathing was shallow and ragged. His mouth felt dry, and he swallowed. Fear welled up inside him and he struggled to suppress it. "All is well, girl. I am here with you," he said, looking into her deep, brown eyes. Soon, his own breathing was following hers, as though they were working together. Teodor felt his heart swell. For the first time he realized he was truly needed. It was a wonderful feeling. He reached into his jacket pocket and rubbed his fingers over his father's silver pin nestled inside.

The barn slowly grew dark as the day came to an end. Someone turned on the aisleway lights, but Amara's stall was still dim, covered in shadows, and quiet. Teodor brought his knees to his chest and wrapped his arms around them, trying to keep warm. Red blotches from the cold garnished his cheeks. His stomach argued with him about the lack of food. But he couldn't leave, dared not leave . . . would never leave Amara just to feed his hunger.

He looked toward the light in the ceiling of the central aisleway. A cobweb, having long since outlived its usefulness and now covered with dust, waved at him. He focused on its gentle movement and felt comforted. This was a new experience, and newness was always hard for him. Any source of comfort was welcome.

Teodor listened to the sounds in the barn. The mare in the next stall noisily munched on her hay. Beyond that, he heard groans from mares in labor and the muffled voices of the men assigned to watch over them. Occasional footfalls moved down the aisle in two-beat clicking sounds, boots against bricks. Stall doors slid on metal tracks.

Sometime in the middle of the night, Amara let out her own long groan and tossed her head toward her swollen belly. A creamy fluid ran out of her vagina and down her hind legs. She folded her front legs and laid down. She rolled over on her side, and Teodor watched as the mare's body convulsed. Her breathing became more rapid, and her body convulsed again.

Teodor felt his heart start to pound. *Is she alright? Is this normal?* Teodor moved over to her head and started stroking her face. Her nostrils flared with each tortured breath. On occasion, she lifted her head and looked toward her swollen belly.

She dropped her head back down and her eyes widened, now exposing the white around the deep brown iris. Her body was wracked with another deep convulsion. Amara groaned as a balloon-like sac appeared and was pushed out the opening of the birth canal below her black tail. The fluid in the sack was clear and Teodor instinctively knew this was good. Another push by the mare and two tiny hooves, one slightly ahead of the other came out.

Teodor smiled. "You're doing it, girl. You're doing it."

Amara lifted her head and looked Teodor in the eye before collapsing her head back into the straw. She breathed rapidly and the boy did the same. Breath for breath, boy and horse breathed in unison.

Teodor waited for what seemed too long a time. He felt perspiration rise on his forehead despite the winter chill inside the barn, his brown curls sticking to his skin. He wiped the sweat off with the sleeve of his jacket, his eyes still glued to Amara. *Is this normal?* He wondered to himself. *Do I need to find Dr. Lessing?* He reached down and stroked her neck. "You're doing good, Amara. I'm here for you." Finally, Amara pushed again, and a dark head emerged, still wrapped in the membranes of the sac that had been its home for eleven months.

Teodor rubbed his sweating palms along his thighs and bit his lower lip, fighting the urge to step toward her haunches and help. He remembered Dr. Lessing told him to leave her alone. So, as much as he wanted to make things go easier for her, he stayed where he was.

Amara lifted her head and looked back toward her tail. With another groan, she lowered her head back down to the straw just as a strong convulsion wracked her sweating brown body. The foal's neck and shoulders slipped out onto the straw. With another hard push, and a gush of fluid, the little horse's hips and back legs came out. In a twisted bundle, the baby lay still behind his mother, still enclosed in the membrane.

At the sight of the foal lying on the straw, Teodor cried out in excitement. "You did it,

Amara. You are such a good girl." He rubbed her neck briskly, still looking back at the dark bundle wrapped in white. Then he paused and lifted his hand from her neck. He caught his breath and narrowed his eyes, staring into the dim light of the stall. Still encased in the amniotic sac, the foal wasn't moving. Teodor clenched his jaw and curled his fists. His heart stopped as panic coursed through his veins. *Is the foal alive?* He could not tell. Pushing up, he hurried to the stall door. "Dr. Lessing, Dr. Lessing."

Rudolf Lessing stuck his head out a stall door a short way down the aisleway. "What is it, Teodor?'

"Come help! The foal is going to suffocate." That was the most words Teodor had strung together ever in his life except when he was talking to a horse. But sometimes emergencies bring out strength that we didn't know we had. Such was the case for Teodor.

Lessing ran to Amara's stall. His knotted eyebrows and wrinkled forehead showed his concern. His lips pressed into a thin, straight line. Teodor turned around and watched Dr. Lessing kneel beside the new foal and gently pull the membrane off the newborn's nose. He lifted the wet head and rubbed the neck. Immediately the baby kicked its gangly legs and shook its head. "He lives!" Lessing said, his voice filled with the ring of rejoicing. He turned to face Teodor, his eyes shining in the darkness. "You did well, boy. It's a colt."

Teodor felt his body relax and he dropped to the straw beside the colt. "A boy," he whispered, a smile cutting his face in half.

"This new little colt should stand within the hour and nurse within two hours," Lessing said as he rocked back on his heels and watched Amara lick her baby. "If that doesn't happen, come get me."

Teodor, his eyes glued to the miracle of life taking place before him, merely nodded.

Chapter 10

Hostau, Spring 1945

The war was finally being felt in the little village of Hostau. Talk around the village square was always about the advancing Soviet forces from the east and the Americans moving toward them from the west. While Hitler and his inner circle continued to spread the propaganda that the Third Reich was succeeding, the villagers knew better.

Agata listened to the talk but dared not respond with her own opinions. One never knew who was loyal to the Nazis. It could be dangerous to appear to be a traitor to the Fatherland. Yet, the honest and brave among them pointed out the numerous losses that the Nazis had suffered. The villagers learned from foreign radio broadcasts that the war was not going as they were being told on German radio. The Red Army was moving toward Berlin from several fronts, signaling that the

Nazis were definitely losing this long war. The American, British, Canadian, Polish, and French forces were squeezing Hitler's army from the west.

For the past several months, refugees from the east passed by the Stud's gates. The people leaving their homelands behind with no more than what they could carry were a pitiful sight. Sadly, they all looked alike. They all appeared tired, dirty, and hungry. Their eyes were empty, their mouths pulled down in a frown. Their clothing was tattered and worn. The animals they brought with them were in even sorrier condition. Fear of the advancing Red Army and seeing the way it was treating those it conquered, drove them west.

Rudofsky allowed the travelers to camp and rest in the Stud's courtyard. Dr. Lessing and his assistant, Dr. Wolfgang Kroll, did their best to help the injured horses. Some were lame, limping on chipped hooves. Others had terrible open sores from ill-fitting harnesses. Still others were just worn out. Even with the men's best efforts, many could not be saved. Each day several were put out of their misery. The vets did what they could with the little time allotted them by the refugees, who were eager to keep moving west. "The Red Army is coming. They are only a few days behind us," they warned the doctors.

One unseasonably nice day in March, Teodor saddled up Witez and took him on a hack. He was now required to keep closer to home as word had gotten out that the Nazis were planting mines in the forest. Happy to be out of the barn and in the soft spring sunlight, Teodor chose to ride along the narrow road that led away from the village. He trotted Witez around a bend in the lane. Just ahead, spanning the width of the road, Teodor saw a group of what appeared to be Russian soldiers. There were about two dozen men, and they were moving toward him.

Teodor stopped, facing the group of men who were on horseback. They were approximately a half kilometer (a third of a mile) down the road. The stallion raised his head and tail and let out a loud snort from his flared nostrils. Teodor felt a tremor shoot down his body. Witez felt it, too. He turned Witez around and squeezed his calves. The horse sprang forward into a gallop. They flew down the road toward the Stud. Glancing back over his shoulder, the boy saw the soldiers following him. Teodor urged his horse on faster. Witez, trained as a racehorse while in

Poland, responded immediately and easily outran them.

Teodor turned into the courtyard and leaped from his horse.

"Dr. Lessing! Dr. Lessing!" Teodor called, gasping for breath.

The vet stepped out of the barn, his face a portrait of concern. "What is it, Teodor?"

"Russians. Russians on the road," Teodor breathed out while pointing back the way he came.

Rudolf Lessing grabbed Witez's reins. "Go to Rudofsky's office in the castle and tell him what you saw."

Teodor clenched his jaw and nodded before setting off at a run. As he headed toward the castle, he heard the clicking sound of hoofbeats entering the courtyard.

Rudofsky was sitting at his desk working on the copious records that he kept on each horse. Hearing three gentle taps in rapid succession on his door, he looked up. "Yes? Please enter."

Teodor sucked in his breath and opened the door. Looking down at his shaking hands, he stepped into the room.

Rudofsky immediately recognized Witez's groom. "Well, what is it?" he said.

"Russians, sir."

"What are you talking about?"

"Russians in the yard."

Rudofsky caught his breath and jumped up from his chair. "Are you sure about this?" he said.

Teodor nodded. "I saw them myself. Come quickly."

Rudofsky hustled to his office window and looked across the gardens to the Stud. "Cossacks," he exclaimed. "What can this mean?" He grabbed his hat and his favorite accessory, his leather whip, and ran out the door. Teodor was on his heels. Rudofsky didn't slow down until he came to a halt in front of the group of soldiers sitting upon their sturdy Anglo-Kabarda mounts.

Teodor stepped to the side of the stallion barn and hid in the shadows. His hand reached into his pocket where he found his father's silver pin. He rubbed it rapidly between his thumb and first finger as he looked to the ground and listened to the exchange.

The visiting officer leading the newcomers dismounted and approached the German officer in charge of the Stud. "I am Prince Amassov," said the young, handsome visitor in flawless German. He had pale blond hair and striking blue eyes and wore a variation of the gray field officers' uniform that Rudofsky wore.

However, the unit badge on his left sleeve confirmed that he was indeed a Cossack, part of the division recruited by the German Army to fight in the war.

The Cossacks were a people inhabiting the lands in southern Russia and Ukraine. They were known for their horsemanship and military skills. Sadly, they had suffered oppression under Stalin's rule. In hopes they might be given independence, thousands of their men joined the German army when the Wehrmacht conquered their lands and promised them privileges for fighting for them. Now that it was obvious that Germany was losing the war, they were hoping to surrender to the Americans.

"Where have you come from?" Rudofsky asked.

"From Poland," the prince responded. "We have brought our families and our horses with us. We have come seeking protection from the Red Army, which would most assuredly execute us as traitors if they were to get their hands on us."

Rudofsky removed his cap and rubbed his fingers over his bald head. "That is asking much of us. Our supplies and facilities are already stretched to the maximum."

The prince stood his ground, his eyes narrowing, his jaw set, a scowl that would be hard to dislodge covered his face. This combat-toughened soldier was not going to be turned away.

Adding another 178 horses to the mix, Rudofsky now had to manage a stable of more than six hundred horses, as well as find shelter for the Cossack refugees. It seemed his role as commander of a large breeding operation had now expanded to nursemaid for displaced families. Though he was technically still under the command of Gustav Rau, it seemed the order was crumbling, and he simply had to make decisions in the best interests of the horses and to the best of his ability.

Chapter 11

Hostau, Mid- April 1945

Rudofsky and Lessing were men who devoted their lives to caring for the horses in their charge. But they were not the only horsemen to frequent the Stud at Hostau. On several occasions, a Luftwaffe Colonel named Walter Holters visited. The Luftwaffe was the aerial-warfare branch of the German Wehrmacht. But clearly, this man's heart was firmly planted on the ground with the horses. Every chance he was afforded, he visited Hostau. He noticed the number of horses and refugees continuing to swell.

"How are you managing all the extra horses and refugees that descend upon you?" the Colonel asked.

"It has been difficult, to say the least," Rudofsky said. "My vets keep busy trying to help their poor animals. Our feed is stretched to the limit. However, some of them, especially the Cossacks, are very knowledgeable and helpful in caring for all the horses."

Holters nodded but didn't respond.

During his frequent visits, Holters walked with Rudofsky around the paddocks, admiring the stallions. He spent hours by the pasture fences watching the mares and foals.

On one such occasion, Holters happened to be on the grounds of the Stud when Teodor was exercising Witez in the arena. He stopped and turned to Rudofsky. "I always dreamed of being able to ride like that."

"Yes, the boy has talent, that is for sure," Rudofsky said. "He is rather peculiar, however. I can barely get a word out of him."

"Well, he doesn't seem to have a problem communicating with the stallion."

One day in mid-April, Holters made a surprise visit to Rudofsky's office. He stepped in the room unannounced. "Colonel Rudofsky," he said.

Startled, Rudofsky jerked his head up from where he was bent over his ledgers. "Colonel, I wasn't expecting you."

Holters looked around then shut the door firmly behind him. "I have come with the most serious of requests."

Rudofsky motioned for the man to sit down in a chair, which the officer gladly obliged. "What is it you desire of me?" Rudofsky said.

Holters was smartly dressed in his air force officer's uniform. He was around fifty years of age and sported a small toothbrush mustache similar to Hitler's. He removed his wire-rimmed glasses and rubbed his eyes before speaking.

"I want to inform you that Vienna has fallen to the Ivans," Holters began.

Rudofsky recognized the slang term the German army used for the Soviet soldiers. He sucked in his breath. "That is disturbing news."

"Not only that," Holters continued, "the Red Army is just outside Pilsen. They are only sixty kilometers away. They could be here any day."

Rudofsky slid his chair back and stood. His jaw was clenched, and he clasped his hands behind his back as he turned to look out the window toward the Stud. His Stud. His horses.

Holters stood and joined him at the window. "I don't need to tell you what this means for the horses."

Rudofsky pressed his lips tightly together and knit his eyebrows.

Holters continued. "You must save the horses. You must contact the Americans. They are close. Very close. Just a mere fifteen kilometers away in Bavaria. If you could deliver the horses to the Americans, their lives would be spared."

Rudofsky turned to Holters. "You are asking me to commit treason!"

"I am asking you to save the horses."

Chapter 12

Hostau, Late April 1945

On April 20, 1945, Hitler's fifty-sixth birthday, the Nazis held a final propaganda effort throughout the areas they still held. Hostau was in the region known as Sudetenland, as three-fourths of the inhabitants were Sudeten Germans. That didn't mean that the local Czechs viewed them as anything but interlopers.

For this last-ditch effort to convince the people that Sudetenland was still German, parades were hastily organized, banners were hung from the buildings, and soldiers marched through the streets.

Lieutenant Colonel Hubert Rudofsky did an impressive riding performance on one of the Lipizzaner stallions in an outdoor arena surrounded by red-and-black banners bearing the Nazi swastika. He never dreamed at the time that it would be his last opportunity to ride one of the magnificent horses.

But in Hostau, all this pomp and circumstance did little to convince the people that anything but failure awaited them. The feeling of peace and safety had fled the village. Fear was ubiquitous. Hostau was slowly suffocating, being squeezed from both sides.

Even the horses seemed to sense it. And for the men at the Stud, the concern was for the horses. What was to become of their beautiful charges?

Teodor spent most of his time in Witez's stall brushing his shiny brown coat and combing his silky black mane. He softly whispered words of comfort to his horse as the stallion munched contently on his hay. The boy moved to Witez's tail and started picking out pieces of straw from the long, black hairs. The peace and quiet he was enjoying was suddenly interrupted when the stable door slammed shut and two sets of boots tapped on the bricks of the aisleway, accompanying the sound of tense voices. Teodor paused his grooming and listened.

"I was hoping the Americans would get here first," said one man whom Teodor recognized as Dr. Lessing.

"They were advancing rapidly, but I have been informed that just a few miles from the border they have come to a halt," Rudofsky responded.

"But why?"

"Only God Himself knows."

"Are the Allies divvying up the countries?" asked Lessing. "And if so, who gets Czechoslovakia? Who gets the Stud?"

"That I do not know. I have made my case with the Commandant concerning the danger the horses are in, but I have been told in no uncertain terms that to surrender the horses to the Americans was out of the question. They are the property of the Third Reich and are to remain so. I was even threatened that such talk was treasonous and would not be tolerated," replied Rudofsky, his whip rhythmically tapping the side of his knee-high leather boots.

"Then we must find our own way to save the horses," Lessing said.

The voices became too soft for Teodor to understand as the men moved farther away. The boy rested his head against Witez's flank and closed his eyes. He reached his hand into his pocket and rubbed the silver pin. He knew one thing: wherever Witez would go, he would go, too.

A few days later, Rudofsky was sitting at his desk in the castle. Suddenly a loud detonation caused the leaded windows to rattle in their metal frames. Rudofsky's first impulse was to duck, but he forced himself to stand and run to the door. Flinging it open, he rushed down the hallway to the front entrance. Pulling open the heavy wooden doors, he stepped outside in time to see a black, swirling plume of smoke rising from the paddock area of the stud. His heart stopped.

Teodor had just clipped Witez in the crossties, getting ready to groom him, when the artillery fire hit. Witez whinnied and reared in the crossties. The other horses who were still in their stalls started kicking at the walls. Teodor could hear the horses screaming in the paddocks outside. But his only concern was Witez.

"Easy boy, easy boy," he said, grabbing the dangling lead rope. Teodor had just calmed Witez when another ripping sound filled the air and another shell hit the ground, landing in the courtyard. Grooms came running into the barn, their arms covering their heads. "Take cover! Take cover," one shouted.

By a pure stroke of luck, no horses were in the paddocks where the artillery hit. But one thing was now certain: the war had come to Hostau.

Chapter 13

2nd Cavalry Headquarters, Bavaria, April 1945

While Rudolf Lessing and Hubert Rudofsky remained busy caring for and worrying about the horses in Hostau, Colonel Holters was executing a plan of his own. With a white strip of cloth tied to the antenna of his black Mercedes staff car, Holters had his driver take him right to the front door of the enemy. But his plan was not to surrender. Instead, he demanded to see the commanding officer. Fortunately for him, the commanding officer was Hank Reed, the horse lover. The pictures Holters presented to him of magnificent horses, many of mares with foals at their sides, immediately caught Reed's attention.

With photos in hand, Reed stared at the images. "Where did you get these photos?" he inquired.

"I took them myself," Holters said in excellent English. "Those horses are why I have come to talk with you today. The horses are in a little village, called Hostau, just fifteen kilometers from here. If you don't do something immediately, they will be lost to the Soviet Army that is, even now, advancing toward them."

"They are truly beautiful," said Reed, his heart pained at the thought of his own horses back in Virginia.

"At the Stud in Hostau are the Lipizzaner brood mares from the Spanish Riding School in Vienna as well as Lipizzaner stallions from Italy and Yugoslavia. Additionally, there are nearly two hundred of Europe's most famous racehorses and a hundred of the finest Arabian stallions. I don't need to tell you what will become of them if the Soviets get to them first."

"I must ask," Reed interjected. "Why are these horses there?"

"An equine expert, by the name of Gustav Rau, convinced the Nazi leadership he had the skills to develop the perfect warhorse. The Hostau Stud was selected as the site for his breeding experiments . . . some results were good, others not. In any case, with the collapse of the Eastern front in late 1944, the breeding program was abruptly halted by the leadership in Berlin. Horses that were selected for the program in Poland and Ukraine were sent to Hostau for safekeeping. They have been there ever since."

Holters proceeded to tell Reed about his own unit that he had moved to a hunting lodge in Dianahof, and of the valuable cache of military records hidden there. These records would all be given to the Americans if they would help rescue the horses from Hostau. Holters stood and extended his hand. "I would like to propose a deal," he said, his face showing no emotion, only determination. "I will surrender the information I possess if you will get the horses out of Hostau. In addition, the Allied POWs at the Stud can be rescued simultaneously."

Reed listened to the German's proposal. "Hmmm. Not an easy task and not one I have the power to perform. The ultimate authority who can decide the fate of the horses is not me, you see. That belongs to my commander, General George Patton. I'll have to investigate this further and make contact with him if possible." Reed rose from his chair and took Holters' proffered hand. As the two men shook hands, Reed continued. "We have a bit of luck on our side, however. General Patton is a devoted horseman, having ridden in the Olympics. In addition, he has a deep hatred for

Stalin and his communist regime. If anyone will give approval for this mission, it will be him."

Thus, without Luftwaffe Colonel Walter Holters, the horses in Hostau would have met an unspeakable fate. Instead, the wheels were set in motion for a dramatic but challenging rescue.

Chapter 14

Hostau Stud, April 25, 1945

On the night of April 25th, Rudolf Lessing was summoned to Lieutenant Colonel Rudofsky's office. Curious about the purpose of the meeting, the vet hurried across the yard and into the castle. Rudofsky didn't make him wait for an explanation.

"A few days ago, I received a visit from Colonel Holters. He warned me that the Soviet Army is just a little over sixty kilometers away, outside Pilsen. They could be here in a day or two."

"What can we do?" Lessing said, wiping the perspiration from his forehead. "You have already been told we cannot surrender the horses."

Rudofsky lifted a communique from his desk and began reading.

I have arranged for the safe passage of the horses over the border to Bavaria. However, this must be kept completely confidential for I don't know who can be trusted. There is the threat of betrayal everywhere. Send one of your officers to meet me at the woodsman's cottage in the forest near the border. I have marked the location on the map included in this message. The man is German and can be trusted to help us. Keep your emissary off the road as I do not want him to be discovered. But send him immediately. Again, tell no one.

Signed,
Colonel Walter Holters

Lessing's mouth dropped open. His eyes widened. "What can this mean?"

"I do not know. I only know what is written here."

"But how can we surrender and move hundreds of horses without suspicion? We'll never get away with it. This is suicide," Lessing said, thinking of his wife and child.

"I have a plan. We won't surrender the horses; we will let the Americans conquer Hostau."

"What?" Lessing asked, pacing back and forth in front of the large desk.

"Just hear me out."

Lessing loosened the top button on his uniform and sat down in a chair.

Rudofsky began relaying to the vet the plan he had concocted. Lessing's eyes got bigger by the minute.

"And when do you want me to leave?" he asked once his commanding officer had completed reciting his plan.

"Tonight. And take that peculiar boy with you."

Teodor was asleep in his cot, dreaming of galloping Witez through the meadows around Hostau. He was awakened by a shake of his shoulder. Opening his eyes, he saw Rudolf Lessing leaning over him. Teodor shot up. "Witez! Is something wrong?"

Lessing put a finger to his mouth and looked around at the other grooms sleeping on their cots. "Shhhh," he said. "Get dressed quickly. We are going for a ride."

Teodor said nothing, though his mind was racing with confusion. His routine was being disrupted and he was struggling to keep control. But, as hard as it was, he obeyed. He pressed his lips together in a tight line and hastily threw on his twill riding breeches, his riding boots, and a warm jacket. He grabbed his father's silver pin from the little table beside his cot and shoved it in his pocket.

By the time Teodor reached the stallion barn, Dr. Lessing had both Witez and Indigo in crossties and was tacking them up.

"I'll explain as we ride," he said over his shoulder as he tightened Indigo's girth.

When both horses were ready, the man and the boy led their mounts into the stable yard. Witez bumped Teodor's shoulder as they walked as if to ask him what was going on. The boy rubbed his horse's face and neck before springing into the saddle.

The night air was crisp and cold, and a slight breeze played with the new leaves on the linden trees as they rode down the drive and through the gates. Both horses were feeling frisky, prancing and snorting, sensing that something was amiss. They were never disturbed during their nighttime rest. This was different. This was something to worry about!

Teodor did his best to keep himself calm so that he could help Witez. But he didn't understand what was going on, either. He looked over at Dr. Lessing riding beside him. The vet's face was hard, his eyebrows knotted and his jaw set, as his eyes moved quickly from one side of the road to the other.

As they left the village, the narrow road heading west entered the thick forest. Lessing led the pair off the road. They began winding their way between the trees and brush. The trees blocked what little light the moon provided, and Teodor squinted to better see what was ahead. He couldn't hear anything but the soft hoof falls of the horses, their loud breathing, and an occasional cracking branch beneath their feet. The forest around him felt ominous. Even the silence felt threatening.

Once they were deep in the forest and far from Hostau, Lessing pulled up his horse and turned to face Teodor. "Boy, we are on an important assignment from Colonel Rudofsky," he began, his voice hushed. "I must tell you that it could be very dangerous."

Teodor sat still and stiff, wide-eyed, and stared at the ground.

"We are going to try to save the horses. But to do so, we must find the Americans and convince them to help us."

Teodor reached his hand in his pocket and rubbed the silver pin.

Chapter 15

The Bohemian Forest, Later That Night

The night was long and seemed to get colder the farther into the forest they rode. They kept their ears tuned for any sounds of the German troops that were patrolling the border between Bavaria and Czechoslovakia. Their destination was a woodsman's cottage some twelve kilometers, or over nine miles, away if the information they had been given was correct.

At one point, an owl swooped down, just missing their heads and startling the horses. It let out a loud hoot before flying back up into the canopy of fir branches. Teodor rubbed Witez's neck. "It's okay, boy," he whispered.

It was the darkest part of the night when Lessing stopped Indigo again. A rustic cabin sat in a clearing in front of them. Lessing leaned over and whispered. "This is where I was told to meet Colonel Holters. He is supposed to take us to the Americans."

The two horsemen stayed under the cover of the forest for several more minutes while Lessing surveyed the surroundings. Then he dismounted and handed his reins to Teodor. "Stay here while I check things out."

Teodor watched, his heart pounding, as Dr. Lessing walked across the clearing and to the front door of the cabin. The vet raised his fist and tapped lightly on the door. Within a few seconds, the door opened, and a bearded older man appeared.

"State your business," he said, his voice gruff.

"I am the veterinarian from the Hostau Stud that was sent to meet Colonel Holters."

"He is no longer here. He feared you were not coming so he left. You will have to go on without him."

Teodor watched as Rudolf Lessing removed his cap and ran his fingers through his blond hair. Then, as though resolving himself to his duty, he replaced his cap, lifted his chest, stuck out his jaw, and said, "Can you point us the way to the Americans?"

Glancing over Lessing's shoulder to where Teodor sat astride Witez and held Indigo's reins, he said, "Let me put your horses in my barn and you can take my motorcycle. It will be easier going on the road."

"We have been instructed to stay off the road," Lessing said, concerned about the German patrols he had been told about.

"No need to worry tonight. The road is clear between here and the border. You'll be safe until you reach the American checkpoint. Then it is up to you to explain why you are there."

Within a few minutes, Witez and Indigo were bedded down in the dilapidated but cozy barn behind the woodsman's cottage. They seemed happy to be rid of their tack as they munched quietly on some hay, old and dusty as it was.

The woodsman filled the tank on his rusted BMW motorcycle with precious gasoline, and Lessing and Teodor climbed aboard. Lessing shifted into drive and twisted the throttle. The small motorcycle lurched suddenly forward, nearly unseating Teodor. The young boy grabbed the vet's coat and held on.

Lessing struggled to keep the bike upright in the thick, slippery mud that covered the narrow, tree-lined road leading to the border with Bavaria. Teodor, still clinging to the vet, wished he was on the back of Witez instead of this noisy, wobbly machine. He closed his eyes and tried to keep his breathing slow and even.

A few kilometers down the road, they arrived at a roadblock. Lessing stopped the motorcycle and placed his left booted foot on the ground to brace it. "I think we have arrived at the border," he said to Teodor.

Just as he spoke, they heard the cock of a rifle. "Who goes there?"

Teodor looked at the ground. Lessing looked straight ahead and smiled. The American accent told him this was not a native German.

"There are two of us. We have come to surrender."

Colonel Hank Reed leaned over a table covered with maps as he debated his next move. A few days before, he and his men of the 2nd Cavalry, with their heavy tanks, had taken over the village of Vohenstrauss in southern Germany. Now he was analyzing the next assignment he just received: seize a hunting lodge called Dianahof and the valuable information hidden there. Holters' visit had made what could have been a very dangerous mission, successful.

While Reed's captains were busy completing their assignment with the assistance of Holters, an army jeep squealed into the yard, sending splatters of mud and debris in all directions. Two American soldiers of the 2nd Cavalry division jumped out of the front. They pushed back their seats. A young man in a German Army uniform and a young boy in riding clothes climbed out.

Teodor bit his lip and silently followed Dr. Lessing across the yard. All around them were signs of war: damaged buildings, rubble on the ground, tanks and jeeps in various states indicating they had seen far too much war. The two enemy soldiers led them into an old farmhouse. The building smelled of smoke and mold. The old wallpaper was faded and peeling. The glass on the windows was so dirty, it barely let in any light. But the parlor they entered was surprisingly neat and tidy, having been swept and dusted recently.

Standing in the parlor, the soldiers told them to wait. Lessing placed his arm around Teodor's shoulder. "It will be alright, Teodor," he said as he felt the boy stiffen. Teodor said nothing, but his mind was a whirl of confusion. He didn't understand how all of this translated into saving Witez.

After several minutes, the soldiers came back. "Colonel Reed will see you, now," one said as he motioned them out the door. "Follow us."

They walked down a dark hallway and through a narrow door at the end that stood ajar. Inside the room, a man stood behind a desk. His arms were folded across his broad chest. He was of average height but built solidly. His face was round, clean-shaven and kind. Teodor glanced up at him and immediately felt safe.

He spoke first. "I am Colonel Reed. I understand you want to share some interesting information with me."

Dr. Lessing stepped forward and pulled out some pictures from his front pocket. He dropped them on the desk. Reed picked them up. His eyebrows knotted and he tilted his head. "I have seen these horses. Hostau, I presume?"

Unaware of Holters' visit and the agreements the two Colonels had made, Lessing explained in broken English. "I have come from the Hostau Stud. These are just a few of the horses in my care. The horses are in danger. I have come to request your help rescuing them."

Reed looked at the young man before answering. "Are you aware that I have met with your Colonel Holters?"

Lessing stepped back in surprise. Shaking his head, he replied, "No. My orders were to meet up with Colonel Holters, but he was not at the rendezvous spot. Thus, we came here on our own."

"Your Colonel Holters has been here, and the first part of our plan is, even as we speak, being executed. If it is successful, we will attempt to save your horses. Though I don't know how at this point."

"Sir, if I may, offer a proposal."

"Of course. Proceed."

"It would be considered treason for us to simply hand over the horses to you. They are the property of the Third Reich," said Lessing.

"Stolen property," Reed interrupted.

Lessing sucked in his breath then nodded. "Stolen property. In any case, we, who have been caring for them and the large number of prisoners of war assisting us, would be in grave danger, especially several Cossacks who want to defect along with members of the Allied forces who are prisoners of war. It must appear that you take possession of Hostau. We will not resist. In fact, few of the villagers are armed."

Reed consulted a map on a table beside his desk. Finding Hostau, he looked up. "The village is fifteen kilometers over the Czech border. Is that right?"

Lessing nodded.

Teodor rubbed his silver pin. His eyes were downcast. He listened intently trying to make sense of the English the men were conversing in.

A soldier entered the room and announced to Reed that dinner was ready.

"Awww. That is welcome news," Reed said. Turning to Lessing, he added, "I'm sure you and the boy could use a warm meal. Follow me."

Teodor and Lessing were seated at a large table in the dining room of the farmhouse. Colonel Reed sat at the head, Lessing to his right and Teodor on the vet's other side. Two new men had joined them at Reed's request. One was named Captain Stewart. He was young and handsome and had a ready smile. Teodor found himself glancing across the table to look at the man's friendly face. He caught the new man wink at him, and he stifled a smile. It soon became apparent that Stewart had been invited to help with the language, he being fluent in both English and German. Whenever there was any confusion, Stewart stepped in to clarify.

The other man was only slightly older. The freckle-faced Irishman, named Bill Quinlivan, was the commander of the 2nd Platoon. His demeanor was that of a toughened warrior, stern and serious. But Reed knew he was a fellow horse lover and would want to be involved in such an important rescue.

Colonel Reed started the discussion once the meal was complete. "I must inform you that your horses are in territory that has been granted to the Soviets," Reed began, addressing the German. "But I can tell you that if you bring your horses through the forest to the American line, I will guarantee their safety and move them back from the front line."

Lessing wiped his mouth with his napkin and placed it beside his empty plate before speaking. "Colonel, I appreciate your kind offer, but that simply won't work. We are in the middle of foaling season. Half the mares are heavy with foal. The other half have youngsters by their sides. It is simply not possible to bring the horses here in the condition they are in."

Reed scratched the stubble on his chin and sighed. Teodor sat in silence, dabbing at the last of the gravy with a roll.

Dr. Lessing spoke up again. "I would like to readdress the proposal I made earlier. Send your men to Hostau and occupy the Stud. We will not fight you." Dr. Lessing looked into Reed's eyes expectantly.

For several minutes Reed stared back, not responding. He chewed on his lower lip and drummed his fingers on the table. He took a deep breath and said, "You are asking me to put my men and equipment in grave danger. Not only are you asking me to go against the agreement we have with Stalin's Army, but we would also risk facing the two German Panzer units patrolling the area."

Lessing nodded, still not taking his eyes from Reed. "For me, it's a simple choice: surrender to the Americans, or let the Russians kill the horses and most likely the Germans who have cared for them and the prisoners of war who have worked alongside us."

Reed sat back in his chair, closed his eyes, and rubbed his temples. Lessing watched and waited. Teodor reached for his silver pin.

A clock bonged the hour, and the wind blew a door shut somewhere in the farmhouse. The three men and the peculiar boy sat in silence, waiting for Reed to speak.

At last, Reed said, "You have come to the right person, Herr Lessing. If ever there was a horse lover, it is I. I will send Captain Stewart back to Hostau with you." Reed paused and smiled at Stewart. "He's a horseman from the great state of Tennessee. He will negotiate with your Colonel Rudofsky and prepare the village for our 'invasion.' I will send First Lieutenant Quinlivan and his platoon to Hostau twenty-four hours later." Reed paused and stared at Lessing, his expression stern. "I repeat, we will be twenty-four hours behind you. See that all is in order when we arrive, and that Stewart is returned to us safely."

An American officer's uniform was hastily assembled for Stewart. Reed penned a letter giving him authority to negotiate with Colonel Rudofsky for possession of the horses in and around Hostau. It was hoped that the letter would get the German officer escorting an American officer through the German checkpoints on the road leading into the village.

The woodsman's motorcycle had been confiscated at the border when Lessing and Teodor surrendered. Thus, late at night on April 26, 1945, two army officers and a young boy *walked* through the American checkpoint and into enemy territory on a mission to save Witez and the horses at Hostau.

Chapter 16

On the Road to Hostau the Next Night

It was another cold, Bavarian night. The moon was now full, and dark shadows dissected the narrow dirt road as it wove through the forest. The men and boy walked swiftly, heading to the woodsman's house to retrieve Indigo and Witez.

It must have been an hour later that the smell of burning wood signaled they were close. As they stepped into the clearing the moonlight reflected off the swirl of gray smoke rising from the stone chimney. It was a welcome sight.

Lessing rapped his knuckles on the rough wood of the door. A few minutes later the old man answered. Seeing the American soldier, he sucked in his breath and stepped back. "Is it safe?" he asked in German under his breath.

"Yes. This is Captain Stewart. He is going to help us save the horses. We will take Indigo and Witez back to Hostau. The boy will have to walk."

"And my motorcycle? What has become of that?"

Lessing sighed. "I'll have to deal with that later."

Teodor wrapped his coat snuggly around him as he watched his beloved Witez being mounted by a stranger. Witez snorted but stood obediently as Stewart placed a foot in the stirrup and swung his right leg over the stallion's back like the seasoned equestrian that he was. Settling in the saddle, he picked up the reins and said, "Nice horse."

"That's an understatement," Lessing said, his eyes roaming over Stewart's position, evaluating the man's skills. "Let's go, Reed didn't give us much time." Giving Indigo a squeeze with his calves, he moved forward.

Teodor stood in the clearing and watched his horse move away. The boy's breathing was rapid. The fingers of his left hand rubbed the silver pin in his pocket. Once the men on horseback disappeared into the trees, he started walking.

Weaving his way through the dense Norway spruce and thick underbrush was hard going. The trees stood like immovable sentries, trying to stop him at every turn. He kept searching the darkness around him, unsure of what might be hiding behind a tree or bush, ready to jump out at him. Every rustle of a branch or snap of a twig sent a wave of fear through him, and his fingers searched for his pin in the bottom of his coat pocket. All the same, he trudged along, hoping no shadowy phantoms would reach out to grab him. He tried to stay focused on his mission. Witez needed saving, and he would make sure he was the one to do it.

Though he was sure he was going in the correct general direction, Teodor had no idea how far he had come, moving in a zig-zag pattern as he was doing. He ran along the labyrinthine trails made by deer or loose cattle, going first one way then the other. Suddenly, he stopped. Every hair on the back of his head began to stand. He heard voices ahead. The male voices were laughing and speaking in German. He caught the unpleasant odor of cigarettes. As he moved closer to the sounds, lights became visible, casting eerie shadows through the forest. Hiding behind a tree, he peeked around. Several German soldiers were sitting on and around a jeep. The vehicle's headlights were pointing toward a barricade set up in the woods.

Teodor's heart pounded in his chest as he scanned the forest for any sign of Witez. Seeing nothing, he felt himself relax, deciding Lessing and Stewart must have ridden safely past the barricade. He decided the letter Colonel Reed had written must have given them safe passage.

Not wanting to take any chances, he whirled to the right and ran—with an "oof"—right into the belly of a very large man. Teodor tilted his head back and looked up into the eyes of a German soldier. He froze and the man grabbed his arms.

"Well, what have we here? Who are you, boy? And what are you doing creeping around in the woods in the middle of the night?" he said while shaking Teodor.

Teodor let loose with a scream that sent the owls and crows aloft. He started flailing and pounding on the man's chest with his fists. Like a wild beast, he started kicking. It had been several years since he had responded to any disruption in his life in such a manner. But this large soldier was getting the full force of what Agata had experienced many times as Teodor grew. But now the boy was bigger and stronger.

The screaming brought the other soldiers crashing through the underbrush.

"What's going on?" shouted one.

The first soldier gritting his teeth and trying to hold on, couldn't answer.

A second soldier came up behind Teodor and wrapped his arms around the boy's waist. The first man let go of his arms and backed away from the flying feet. Teodor kept screaming, flailing his arms, and kicking his legs. The expression on the face of the man holding him showed he was clearly surprised at how strong such a small boy could be. He struggled to hold on while grunting and groaning, but soon dropped him to the ground.

In the blink of an eye, Teodor was on his feet and moving away from the men. One man reached out, catching the hem of Teodor's coat. The wiry boy squirmed and wiggled until the buttons of his coat popped off. He pulled his arms free of his coat and bolted toward the nearest cluster of trees, leaving the soldier holding nothing more than an empty fabric shell.

"Halt!" The soldiers yelled. But there was no stopping Teodor.

Curiously, the brush with near-capture put new heart in Teodor, and he ran with renewed determination. The boy ran through the brush, pushing branches and brambles out of his way.

His face and hands were soon scratched and bleeding. He didn't care. He needed to make sure he was well away from the soldiers.

He ran until he felt he could run no more. Then he did run more!

When Teodor came to a stream, he stopped. He turned to look back to where he had come from. He tried to quiet his panting so he could listen. Cupping his hand to his ear he waited. Silence. There didn't seem to be anyone coming. Confident that he was alone, Teodor bent down at the water's edge and splashed his face, washing off the blood that was trickling down to his collar. He cupped his hands and drank, still listening for any sound, human or otherwise. The cold water made him shiver in the night air, but it brought a level of rejuvenation that Teodor badly needed.

He knew he dare not stop for long, but the short break and the drink was just what he needed to continue. He splashed through the icy water and started running. The fifteen kilometers, or approximately nine miles, proved to be much longer than that due to the convoluted pattern he was running through the forest, necessary as it was to keep out of sight of patrolling Germans. At one point, he heard the drone of an aircraft flying overhead. He crouched behind a large boulder and waited, his heart pounding in his chest. *Is it German or American?* He had no way of knowing nor did he know which he would prefer.

The sun was just coming over the eastern mountains when Teodor reached the edge of town after having run for over three hours, the best he could do in the dark and with such difficult ground to cover. He hurried up the road leading to the two- and three-story buildings, the tall church spire, and the castle.

A German checkpoint was newly set up across the road entering Hostau. Confused and uncertain about what to do, his teeth chattering in the cold, Teodor reached for his father's pin in his pocket. Gone! His coat with the pin inside the front pocket was gone. The soldiers had it and now it would be lost to him forever.

Teodor collapsed in the middle of the road. Shivering, he closed his eyes and started rocking. He twisted his hands in his lap. Slowly, a thought entered his mind. In order to be safe, he needed to avoid detection. Remembering a trail along the edge of the forest he had ridden many times, Teodor pushed himself up and headed to his left. Finding the trail in the pale light of the breaking dawn, he hurried along the path. Once out of sight of the checkpoint, Teodor cut across the field, circumventing the barrier and the German soldiers who manned it. He ran behind the homes and businesses that lined the main street, jogging up the hill. Dogs announced his arrival as he passed their small yards, but he paid them no mind. Pumping his arms to help him run, his heart beat loudly as his breath came in great gulps. He sucked in air through his chapped and swollen lips. He ran up the hill toward the castle. When he reached the welcome gates of the Stud he turned in, picked up speed, and ran between the linden trees. He had only one thing on his mind . . . Witez.

Sliding open the heavy barn doors, he hurried down the aisleway to Witez's stall. Looking between the bars, he saw Witez calmly munching on his morning hay.

"Witez!" was all he said before he collapsed to the ground.

Chapter 17

Hostau, April 27, 1945

Teodor woke to find he was in his cot with his mother sitting beside him.

She reached out to touch his forehead but quickly pulled her hand back when she saw him flinch.

"How are you feeling?"

"Witez?" Teodor asked, his eyes searching the shadows in the room.

"He is fine. Last I saw, he was trotting around his paddock trying to get the attention of the mares."

Teodor smiled. "Teodor's horse."

"Yes. Teodor's horse," Agata said, relieved that her son was back safely from an assignment she had only just learned about. Lessing came to her door early that morning to tell her the bare minimum of Teodor's journey to Bavaria and that he was back safely, sleeping on his cot in the farmhouse. She grabbed a shawl and followed the vet. For several hours, she sat beside her son, waiting for him to awaken. She knew she would not get much information from Teodor, and Lessing had been hesitant to tell her the purpose of their journey . . . only that they were back safely.

Lessing and Stewart, however, were not yet in a position of safety. The vet returned to the castle to tell Rudofsky all that transpired during his mission, eager to inform him that Reed and the Americans agreed to save the horses. To his surprise, Rudofsky did not respond with the anticipated excitement. Instead, his commanding officer had very bad news for him.

"While you were gone, General Schulz arrived in town setting up defenses."

"Yes," replied Lessing, "I was stopped by the sentry, but was able to talk my way through with the help of a letter from Colonel Reed."

Rudofsky raised his eyebrows in surprise. "Very interesting. However, Schulz has been calling for both you and Kroll. For what purpose, I know not. I told him the two of you were visiting the outlying farms, caring for the animals."

Rudofsky wiped his sweating hands on his starched pantlegs and took a deep breath. "He has been assigned with defending Hostau."

"What? That is madness. His little army of young, untrained, soldiers can't compete with what the Americans have to offer in a battle. Not to mention, the danger this puts the horses in."

Rudofsky dropped his head in his hands. "Everything is spiraling out of my control. All I ever wanted to do was take care of the horses. Now, just as we think we have saved them, it appears all is lost."

"No, all is *not* lost," said Lessing, placing his hands on the desk and leaning forward. "I will talk to Schulz myself. Surely, I can reason with him, make him see the best course of action."

"You may go, but realize that you and I, and the American you have brought with you, may be facing our deaths."

Lessing marched out of the castle, his mind a whirl of conflicting thoughts. On the one hand, his duty to the horses required that he do everything possible to save them. In addition, he also desired to keep his wife and little daughter, living near Hostau, safe from the Soviets. It was a heavy burden that he carried into General Schulz's office in the castle that day.

The veterinarian entered the General's office and stood straight and stiff in front of him. Schulz, a small man, dressed in the field-gray uniform with the red and gold collar tabs of a German general, eyed him with a look of suspicion. Lessing took in a deep breath before beginning to speak. He recounted to the General all that had transpired during his negotiations with the Americans. The longer he talked, the redder Schulz's face grew.

Unable to listen any further, Schulz leaped from his chair, knocking it over. "Traitor! You are a traitor," he shouted. "I should have you shot for treason this instant!"

Tired from two days on the road with little sleep or nourishment, Lessing was at his wits end. Lifting his chin and glaring at this man who was his superior, he refused to stand down.

"I am no traitor. But I can see the writing on the wall, and you should be able to as well. At this point, my only desire is to save the horses who I have been assigned to care for." The frustration at the Nazi lies and propaganda he had been putting up with for so long, boiled over, and he continued. "If you can't see that the war is lost, I haven't the power to convince you otherwise. But I will not allow you to put the horses and the people who have been caring for them in danger by engaging in an unwinnable battle." Lessing pressed his lips together, his hands clenched into fists at his sides.

A heavy, ominous silence filled the room. General Schulz had never been spoken to in such an insolent manner during all his military career. Perhaps only his wife had stood up to him with such impudence! At a loss for words, he stared at Lessing.

After several minutes, Schulz cleared his throat and smoothed his shirt. Bending over, he picked up his chair and lowered himself into the seat. Clutching his hands in front of him on the desk he spoke, his voice reflecting the exhaustion and, perhaps, resignation, that he felt. "You will have to state your case to my corps commander."

With no time to waste, Dr. Lessing and Indigo made a mad dash to the German regional headquarters in the ancient castle, Schloss Gibacht, outside the town of Kladrau. It was a journey of thirty-nine kilometers (twenty-four miles) from Hostau. But a journey a tired horse and an exhausted veterinarian needed to take to save the horses and people at

Hostau—to save what little remained whole in this war-torn land.

Chapter 18

Hostau, April 28, 1945

Lessing soon learned a valuable lesson. When politicians and military leaders see a losing end in front of them, they will do anything to keep from carrying the blame. Instead, they will run from taking responsibility. Such was the case as Lessing galloped back to Hostau with a letter in his hand turning all responsibility for dealing with the American invasion and capture of the horses at the Stud back to General Schulz. Passing the buck at its finest.

After heated arguments between Schulz and his officers in front of both Lessing and Stewart, Schulz offered Stewart safe passage back to the American line and the promise there would be no defense of Hostau or the Stud if the Americans arrived. However, their promise only applied to the Wehrmacht, the regular army of Nazi Germany. They could not promise that the SS would not attack.

The SS began as Hitler's personal bodyguards but evolved into the most feared organization in Nazi Germany. The soldiers not only were involved in intelligence-gathering but also ran the concentration camps. As the Nazis saw their loss as inevitable, it was the military arm of the SS, referred to as the "Waffen-SS," that refused to submit. The very mention of the SS in Hostau sent chills down the spines of the villagers.

With limited approval, Lessing and Stewart hurried back through enemy territory to inform Colonel Reed that the rescue was now possible, though there were no guarantees it would be peaceful. Some of the units assigned to help would be traveling through areas where German Panzer tank divisions had been spotted.

It was a thickly overcast day. A heavy mist hung over the ancient fields around Hostau, concealing the thick Bohemian Forest beyond. Teodor was finishing his morning chores and lining up Witez's brushes in the grooming box. The sound of distant gunfire broke the silence of the morning. Teodor's body stiffened as he listened.

Colonel Rudofsky, conducting his morning inspections in the stallion stables, stopped outside Witez's stall and listened. The initial blasts were replaced by the deep resonating sound of explosions. "Stay with Witez," Rudofsky shouted to Teodor as he ran out of the barn.

The sounds continued as the Stud's commander and several grooms and POWs stood in the courtyard.

"Panzers, Colonel," cried a groom in the ominous silence between blasts.

"But where are they coming from? The Americans or the Soviets?" Rudofsky said, straining his ears as the sounds started up again.

"There," one groom called out, pointing to the Northwest.

"The Americans."

Rudofsky started as he heard General Schulz speak beside him, not realizing he was there. Behind his spectacles, Schulz darted a hostile flash of his eyes toward Rudofsky. Then, the General stalked off toward the castle, got into his Mercedes, and commanded his driver to head south, never to be seen in Hostau again.

At that moment, a black horse appeared out of the fog, galloping up the main drive into the

Stud. A very tired and dirty Rudolf Lessing dropped with a thud from his horse. As two grooms stepped forward and took Indigo into the stable, the vet shuffled over to Rudofsky. "They are coming," Lessing choked out as he gasped for breath.

Rudofsky lifted his chin and said, "We must prepare." Turning on his heel, he marched into the barn.

Teodor watched from Witez's stall as Rudofsky, with jaw set and looking straight ahead, walked toward his office, his polished boots clicking on the brick aisleway. The boy slipped out of the stall and silently followed. Rudofsky pushed open his office door and entered the room that was so familiar to him and all his staff. Without looking back, the commander stepped up to the portrait of Adolf Hitler that had stared down at him for so many years. He reached up and removed the picture from the wall.

Teodor gasped. Rudofsky turned and for a moment merely looked at the boy. Then he spoke in a quiet, determined voice. "Lower the Nazi flags and bring them to me."

Teodor turned to obey but was stopped when Rudofsky spoke again. "And replace them with white sheets."

Soon, white makeshift flags were waving in the breeze, welcoming the oncoming saviors.

Chapter 19

Hostau Stud, Later That Day

As the American tanks and vehicles advanced on Hostau, the unorganized and disjointed resistance offered by the few remaining German soldiers failed to stop them. American tanks fired on the western edge of the village, damaging some houses and sending plumes of dust and debris into the air to mix with the fog. The German troops, now leaderless and lacking the commitment to continue fighting a losing battle, began retreating to the other end of town. The horses at the Stud, frightened by the loud sounds, began whinnying and kicking at their stalls. Mares huddled in corners protecting their foals. Teodor stood in Witez's stall, repeatedly stroking the stallion's arched neck.

Suddenly, all became quiet as two men walked down the drive between the linden trees, turned west on the main road, and moved toward the oncoming tanks. A white sheet was stretched between them. Rudofsky and Lessing didn't speak as they moved forward, both men hoping they were doing the right thing.

The tanks and vehicles ground to a halt, their engines idling. Stewart and Quinlivan climbed out of a jeep at the rear and walked to the front. With a smile on his face, Stewart greeted Lessing and Rudofsky. Quinlivan remained stoic. The two Germans clicked their heels together and gave a sharp military salute.

A short time later, the Stars and Stripes was hoisted up the flagpole in the middle of the town where the Nazi flag once flew. Old Glory unfurled in the breeze just as the clouds parted and a beam of sunlight split the sky and lit the flag.

There was no time to celebrate. A feeling of urgency filled every heart, both German and American. The Americans were ordered to work swiftly to get the horses and POWs back over the border. The Germans feared the advancing Red Army. Preparations had already begun at the Stud with tack and equipment having previously been packed in crates. Feed was bagged. The German POWs that Quinlivan's men captured were securely locked away in cellars and kept under constant guard. Such was the state of affairs in the little village of Hostau.

A tour of the stables by the Americans revealed three hundred horses. Many more were housed at facilities in three nearby villages. Rudofsky and his grooms had been caring for over five hundred horses.

Upon completion of the tour, Quinlivan and Stewart turned to one another.

"I had no idea of the enormity of this task," Quinlivan said.

Stewart let out his breath with a huff. "Can we possibly do this?"

"We must," was all Quinlivan could say.

Chapter 20

Hostau, April 29, 1945

Colonel Hank Reed passed by the sentries guarding the road into and out of Hostau. He gave his men a sharp salute from where he sat beside his driver. The jeep proceeded to the courtyard of the Stud and came to a halt in front of several Germans, each holding the lead rope of a magnificent horse. Lieutenant Colonel Rudofsky, dressed in a long gray overcoat, held the lead of a large, white Lipizzaner stallion. Dr. Lessing held his beloved Thoroughbred Indigo. Dr. Kroll stood to one side holding a beautiful Lipizzaner mare with a jet-black foal at her side. Prince Amassov stood beside his favorite bay Anglo-Kabarda horse. And Teodor stood, with eyes downcast, beside the beautiful bay Polish Arabian, Witez.

Reed stepped out of the jeep and faced the men. They gave him a salute which he quickly returned. But his eyes were on the horses standing in front of him. Witez and Teodor caught his eye, and he stepped up to them. "It's good to see you again, Teodor. That's a fine-looking horse you have there."

Lessing translated and Teodor merely nodded. His language skills had already caught the gist of the Colonel's comments.

"And what is your horse's name?" Reed asked.

Keeping his eyes locked on a pebble at his feet, Teodor answered. "Witez II."

"Ahhh. A lovely name for a lovely horse," Reed said, before moving down to stand in front of Rudofsky.

Rudofsky stiffened. He looked beyond Reed who was shorter than himself by a head. Perspiration beaded on his forehead as he faced the man to whom he had surrendered.

"Colonel Rudofsky, can you give me an accurate account of the horses now in your care?"

Lessing handed Rudofsky a clipboard.

Rudofsky flipped through the pages and then looked Reed in the eye. "589, Colonel. There are 247 Lipizzaners, 64 Arabians, 144 Kabardiners, 75 Don horses, and 59 Panje horses. Several have been left in our care by emigrants. The rest have been part of our breeding program."

If Reed was shocked or dismayed by the large number, he didn't show it. "Very good, Colonel. I will be returning to my headquarters to make arrangements to move the horses and the prisoners of war. You will remain here and oversee the evacuation."

Rudofsky's mouth dropped open, and he blinked in surprise. "You mean you're not going to take me as a prisoner?"

Reed laughed. "Should I?"

"I'd prefer that you didn't."

"Well, Colonel," Reed said with a smile, "I need you here to help make this mission a success. If you are willing to do that, it seems you would be more helpful here than in a prison camp."

The work of evacuation began in earnest. Troop carrier trucks were converted to hold horses. These were to be used for the mares who were heavy with foal or those who had just delivered. Grooms and American soldiers, those who could ride, were recruited to run herd on the loose horses. All available vehicles were loaded to overflowing with bags of feed, and crates stuffed with tack and stable equipment.

Colonel Reed made it very clear to Rudofsky that he was not going to be responsible for the Cossacks, their families, and their horses. "They stay here," he instructed firmly. Thus, the Cossacks, being Russian citizens, were to be left to fend for themselves.

The other issue Reed was adamant about was the insistence that Rudofsky accompany the horses to Bavaria—something that the Sudeten German did not want to do. He had lived his whole life in Sudetenland, near Hostau. He owned property there. His aged mother still lived nearby, as did his sister-in-law and nephew. But Reed would not budge, so Rudofsky had no choice but to comply with Reed's orders.

And then there was the matter of Teodor. Other than the night Teodor accompanied Lessing to meet with Colonel Reed, the boy hadn't been out of the village his entire life. Of course, barely into his teenage years, his entire life had not yet been very long. Rudofsky knew Witez would be one of the horses rescued by the Americans. He struggled with what he should do about Teodor. The horse had been cared for by the boy each day since the stallion's arrival in Hostau. The horse trusted him, perhaps even loved him. And, clearly, the boy loved Witez. Magic existed between them; there was no denying that.

Rudofsky decided to address the issue head-on.

Leaving his office in the castle, Rudofsky walked through the castle gardens, now neglected, past the palace wall, and across the courtyard to the stallion barn. Teodor was right where he expected him to be – in Witez's stall.

"Have you gathered all of Witez's tack?" he asked Teodor while standing in the open stall door.

Teodor continued his rhythmic brushing of Witez's tail while nodding in acknowledgment.

"Very good," Rudofsky said. He dipped his chin and rubbed his forehead before continuing. "You realize as soon as we receive orders from Colonel Reed, Witez will be taken by the Americans to Bavaria."

Teodor nodded again.

"Have you considered what you will do then?"

Teodor stopped brushing. "Teodor go with Witez."

"What of your mother? You both need to understand that you may never see one another again."

In a rare sign of emotion, a tear trickled down Teodor's cheek and he buried his face in Witez's flank. He mumbled again, "Teodor go with Witez."

Chapter 21

Hostau, April 30, 1945

On April 30 word reached the Stud that the SS had been spotted in the area and was moving toward Hostau. It wasn't just any SS unit, either. Moving toward them was perhaps the most brutal of them all: a Panzer unit whose stormtroopers' taste for blood and torture was legendary.

The previous December, just as Hitler launched his last-ditch offensive that became known as the Battle of the Bulge, this very unit committed one of the most heinous crimes of the war. A large group of American prisoners of war was massacred in a field outside the small town of Malmedy in Belgium. Machine-gunned and left in the snow, many of those who weren't killed immediately died soon after of exposure or gunshots to the head.

None of the American soldiers tasked with rescuing the horses wanted to face the tanks and artillery of a Panzer unit. But the Germans in Hostau, now essentially prisoners of war themselves, feared the arrival of the SS even more, knowing how loyal these soldiers were to Hitler and the Nazi cause. The Germans would surely be viewed as traitors.

The SS managed to quickly set up a roadblock right along the route the Americans planned to use to get the horses to Bavaria. Two of the SS officers crouched behind trees on a hillside watching Hostau through binoculars. From their location, they could see the American flag floating lazily in the gentle breeze.

"What does that mean?" asked one.

"I have been told that the village has surrendered to the Americans," was the reply.

"The Americans? I thought we were going to face the Red Army."

"Just another twist in this ever-changing war, I guess," said the second with a shrug. "But no matter, American blood spills just as freely as Russian."

In large numbers, the SS troops began moving through the trees toward the village. Fearlessly, they moved forward, firing their rifles. Dressed in camouflage, they moved into the fields, continuing to fire their small arms.

Immediately the villagers, grooms, and POWs, who had been armed by the Americans in case such an event should happen, began firing back. The Americans, Germans, Cossacks, and the POWs from Poland, Britain, and France —a true foreign legion—fought to protect the horses, determined that the SS would not capture them and the village

At the Stud, the horses were in a panic, frightened by the explosions and the constant rattle of small arms. Sudden loud noises would ordinarily send Teodor into a panic. But the boy's focus stayed on calming his horse. He remained in Witez's stall, trying his best to soothe the stallion by rhythmically stroking his neck and rubbing his forehead, while at the same time comforting himself.

Mid-afternoon, after five brutal hours, the fighting at long last stopped. Hundreds of SS lay bloodied and dying across the fields and in the forest. The Americans moved out to collect over a hundred prisoners of war. Mortar fire had started several forest and grass fires, sending black smoke into what should have been a crystal clear, blue sky. The fires needed to be squelched quickly.

While this battle was just ending in little Hostau, another fire was burning several hundred miles to the north. At around 3:30 pm, sitting in his bunker in Berlin next to Eva Braun, his new bride of just a day and a half, Adolf Hitler placed a capsule of cyanide between his teeth. As he bit down, he pulled the trigger on the Walther automatic pressed against his temple. His wife followed his example and also poisoned herself with cyanide. Hitler's followers, or perhaps his rivals, moved their bodies from the bunker, and placed them in the garden. Dousing them with gasoline, they watched their former leader's body get consumed by the flames.

Chapter 22

Hostau, May, 1945

The death of Hitler did not end the war. New Nazi leadership was set to take the reins. The propaganda over the airwaves continued the very next day, assuring the German people that their cause was just, and they would continue to resist the Soviet invasion to the east and the American and British invasion on the west.

Yet, despite all the death, life continued to blossom forth in Hostau as more mares delivered foals. The fields and barns were populated by the black babies beside the white Lipizzaner mares, the gray and brown Arabians beside their like-colored mothers, and the brown and bay Thoroughbreds running circles around their dams.

Captain Stewart was chomping at the bit to get moving. But Rudofsky and his veterinarians, Lessing and Kroll, insisted that the mares and new foals couldn't be moved.

But what of the Soviets? Although they were being kept busy moving on Prague, it wouldn't be long before they would set their eyes on Hostau and its treasure of horses.

Teodor watched as Lessing and Rudofsky paced up and down the barn aisle, conversing in whispers, their faces tense, their fists clenched. The boy listened carefully and learned that Rudofsky desired to stay in Hostau even after the horses had left.

"This is my home. The only home I've ever known," he said to Lessing.

"You must be crazy," Lessing whispered. "The Czechs hate the Germans."

"I'm Sudeten," protested Rudofsky.

"Not in the eyes of the Czechs, you aren't. You're the enemy."

Teodor turned back into the stall. Sitting cross-legged in the corner, he rocked forward and back, forward and back, as he arranged the pieces of straw into parallel lines in front of his legs. No one knew how hard the boy struggled to control his emotions with all the changes and upheaval he was facing. His very survival depended upon order and routine . . . of which little was to be found. He lost himself, or perhaps it would be better to say that he saved himself, in caring for Witez.

Colonel Reed returned to Hostau after an exhausting week spent trying to secure the horses' passage to Bavaria. It had not been easy or pleasant.

Reed, First Lieutenant Bill Quinlivan, who since April 28th had been responsible for security at the Stud, Stewart, and Rudofsky met in the German colonel's office in the castle. Much needed to be discussed, much decided upon.

"My biggest concern is the mares," Rudofsky said. "We need to move those that are still pregnant without inducing labor."

Reed nodded. "I put Quinlivan in charge of devising a plan to move them. Under his direction, we are converting troop carriers to transport them. We will load them in the back of the trucks. It may not be pretty, but it should work."

"It seems the rest of the horses will need to march out. We have been recruiting riders among my staff and grooms, and your men to ride herd," said Rudofsky. "With what we have determined, we will still face a shortfall of experienced riders."

Reed removed his glasses and rubbed his eyes.

Rudofsky hesitated before speaking. "May I make a suggestion?"

"Please do," said Reed.

"I know you previously said that the Cossacks were to remain here. But Prince Amassov has volunteered his men. They are excellent horsemen and have proven to be hard workers in the time they have been here at the Stud."

Reed drummed his fingers on the desk. This added even more horses and people to be moved. His initial thought was to say no.

"Do you trust them?" asked Reed.

"I do," responded Rudofsky. "They are good people."

Reed pursed his lips and slowly nodded his consent.

"We'll need to organize the horses down into manageable groups," said Rudofsky.

"And keep the stallions and mares separated . . . widely separated," added Stewart.

Rudofsky nodded. "I will put Lessing and Kroll in charge of organizing the groups and riders."

After much discussion, it was agreed that Reed would allow the German and Cossack families and personal belongings to come along on this unique horse caravan.

The final issue of concern was where to put the horses once they reached Bavaria. Dr. Kroll, Lessing's assistant, had just returned from touring the farms in the area around Kötzting and Furth im Wald where Reed planned to house the horses. He was called in to join the meeting. His report was far from encouraging.

"The horse accommodations are not satisfactory to house the kind of spirited horses we have here," he began.

"What do you mean?" asked Reed.

"The people are just poor peasants. Their small stables are little more than shacks and cowsheds. The fencing on the pastures is in poor condition," summed up Kroll. "However, over the last two days, I have driven all around the countryside and made negotiations with the owners of the modest estates. By arranging to place two mares here and three there, all over the area, I have found shelter for all our horses."

"Excellent," beamed Reed.

Rudofsky didn't seem as enthusiastic. "What of the pastures?

Kroll shook his head. "The forage is sparse and in poor condition. I estimate that the fields as they are will only support the more than five hundred horses for a couple of weeks."

This was disturbing news to Rudofsky who had always worked to provide the horses with the finest of care, feed, and accommodations. He clenched his jaw and rubbed his hands together.

Reed, noticing Rudofsky's hesitation, added, "Well, for the short term, this will have to do. Our immediate and most pressing goal is to get the horses out of Czechoslovakia. Once they are safely in Bavaria, we will plan our next step."

Chapter 23

Hostau, May 11, 1945

Teodor stepped onto the front stoop of his mother's tall, narrow house nestled in the middle of a row of identical houses. Glancing up, he gazed at the leaded-glass window that marked the location of his bedroom, the window he had often sat in front of as he watched the world go by without him. Now he was living in that world, and it was taking him places he had never dreamed of. Never capable of dreaming of. Never dared to dream of. Were it not for Witez, he might still be living in that room with no dreams at all.

He raised his hand and pressed down on the latch. Pushing the door open, he stepped into the foyer he knew so well. The house was dark and quiet, except for the friendly ticking of the old clock on the mantel. The familiar smell of baking bread wafted from the kitchen and gave Teodor the strength he needed.

He walked silently into the kitchen. His mother was bending over the old, black stove, pulling a loaf of bread out of the oven. Teodor watched her but said nothing, waiting for her to notice him first. He didn't have to wait long.

Agata turned to place the bread on the kitchen table. As she did so, she was startled to see her son standing there. She gasped and nearly dropped the hot pan. "Teodor! You scared me," she said, setting the pan down before clasping her hands to her chest to slow her pounding heart.

For several minutes, there was silence in the room as Agata studied her son and Teodor struggled to find words. The boy felt the anguish inside start to build. The order in his life, which he so deeply craved and required to function, was falling apart. A deep groan arose from within.

Agata rushed forward and extended her hands, afraid to touch. Slowly, Teodor raised his hands and placed them in hers. Tears welled up in Agata's eyes and she did nothing to keep them from overflowing and coursing down her cheeks. She held Teodor's hands as she watched the cloud of confusion wash over her son's face.

Teodor had improved in his ability to communicate while working with Witez, but expressing his emotions was still beyond his skill level. The internal struggle he was feeling was tearing him apart. Could he possibly function without the strength and security of his mother? She had always been his safe harbor as he navigated in the stormy seas of the world around him.

Yet, there was Witez. Witez the healer.

"Teodor go with Witez," he said softly.

Agata dropped one of Teodor's hands as her own flew to her mouth. Did she understand correctly? She knew the Americans were preparing to take the horses. But Teodor? How could this be?

She struggled to slow her breathing. "Are you saying you are going away?'

Teodor nodded.

"Where? For how long?" she managed to stammer.

Teodor looked at her hand still holding his, then shook his head. He truly didn't know how to answer. He had always just lived in the moment, responding to what was right in front of him. Plans and events in the future were completely unknown and unimagined for him. That was not a part of how he functioned. He only understood the here and now.

Agata was facing her own struggles. Protecting Teodor had been her purpose for the past thirteen years. She provided for his physical needs but also did her best to guide him through the unknown world around them, and his unpredictable, and often uncontrollable, responses to it. But then Witez came into his life, into both their lives, and her son changed. It was truly a miracle. But would it be enough?

"Will you let me hug you?" Agata whispered through her tears.

Teodor nodded and for the first time in many years, Agata wrapped her arms around her son. She felt him shudder and then become quiet. His stiff body softened, his shoulders dropped, and he melted into her. Her tears glided steadily down her cheeks, falling into the curls on the top of Teodor's head. Their hearts began beating in unison.

As they parted, something in their hearts told them they would never see one another again. Agata stood in the center of the room, her arms reaching out toward her son. Teodor did not look at his mother, nor did he say anything as he turned and went out the door for the last time.

Chapter 24

Preparing to Escape, May 12, 1945

While Rudofsky continued to oversee the care of the horses, Quinlivan supervised the conversion of American and German trucks into horse vans, and Lessing and Kroll organized the teams of riders, Captain Stewart made sure all the food and supplies were loaded on trucks.

Evacuating a virtual city of four-legged inhabitants was not an easy task.

With Prince Amassov's help, Lessing and Kroll organized those horses that would walk without riders into groups of thirty to eighty. He assigned five or six men to ride herd on each group. Teodor was assigned to ride Witez with a group of thirty-five stallions. He would have the help of several of Amassov's men.

With preparations complete, the last task was the hardest. The pregnant mares and those with new foals at their sides were loaded into the transport trucks that served as makeshift horse vans, being led by grooms up equally makeshift ramps. Many of the mares resisted, but those that were the most cooperative were led in first, giving the reluctant ones enough confidence to follow.

It was decided that the trucks holding the mares would head out first.

Just as the drivers were in the cabs and the engines started, the rumbling of the trucks was overpowered by the deep, bone-rattling roar of tanks coming from the east.

"What is going on?" shouted Reed over the noise of machines and the whinnying of horses. As if in response, a green-painted tank, smoke belching from the rear exhaust pipes, rounded a corner, and came into view.

Several more tanks came around the corner and all ground to a halt. A young Soviet Lieutenant stood up in the open hatch of the first tank, waving and shouting wildly.

Reed commanded his men to hold their fire as he approached the tanks that were sitting on the road, their motors idling. The Soviet officer continued to shout. Reed turned back to Quinlivan and Stewart. "We have anyone who speaks Russian?" Reed said, his fists on his hips and irritation written on his face.

A Cossack soldier rode up on his little Kabarda horse. Saluting Reed he said, "What can I do to help?"

"Ask him what he is doing here," Reed commanded his interpreter.

"He says you must clear the road for the Red Army."

"Tell him we will not do that. We are here on official business."

Back and forth, the conversation went with neither side budging and tempers rising. Reed was certain that the Soviet Army's presence was a great threat to the horses and that if the Reds should get past, the mission to rescue them would fail. He set his mind that they weren't getting past him without a fight.

Soon the column's commander appeared. Stomping back and forth in front of the first tank, his arms flailing in rhythm to his words, he made the same demands.

Lifting his chest, Reed said, "Tell the General that we have taken control of Hostau, and he is now behind American lines." Reed knew this was a stretch as the Yalta agreement gave all of Czechoslovakia to the Soviets. However, that agreement was only to take affect once Germany surrendered. For now, he was going to use all his bluff and bluster to hold his ground. "If you move forward, we will use all our arms and strength to stop you."

For several minutes, the Soviet officers argued back and forth with one another. Suddenly, shouts went down the line and the tanks turned off their engines. An eerie silence followed.

Reed, Quinlivan, and Stewart stood in the road for only a minute more before turning back to the Stud. "Move out," they commanded. Lessing, on Indigo, and Quinlivan and several German officers mounted on horses beside him stepped onto the road. Immediately behind them, Stewart's jeep rumbled to life.

On this beautiful spring morning, with not a cloud in the sky, a great caravan of human and horse refugees began to roll west. Only Hubert Rudofsky and a handful of villagers watched them move down the road. Rudofsky continued to insist to the very last that he would not leave Hostau. Reed decided he didn't want to press the issue and left the Colonel behind.

As the last horse disappeared, a dejected and deflated Rudofsky turned and walked into the village. He stopped at the door of a tall, narrow house. Looking from side to side, he hesitated. He wasn't quite sure why he was here, only that he felt an emptiness he doubted he would ever fill.

In her tidy kitchen, Agata sat at the table, her head bowed. The sound of a knock brought her back from her musings. She arose and went to the door. Opening it a mere crack, she gasped. "Colonel," she stammered. "Can I help you?"

This once strong man, a confident leader, lowered his chin and shook his head.

Agata opened the door further and beckoned him in.

He entered the tidy sitting room but remained standing. He slowly turned to face Agata. "This war has taken everything from us," he began. "I am a man without a country, a man without a purpose. Without the horses, I'm not sure who I am anymore. I guess I just thought you would understand."

Agata dropped down on the well-worn couch, put her face in her hands, and cried.

Chapter 25

The Road to Bavaria

Teodor and Witez were in the second group of horses. Five riders, including Teodor, were in charge of herding thirty-five spirited, impulsive stallions. Many were white Lipizzaners, and the others were black or bay Thoroughbreds and Arabians. Witez's calm nature helped keep the unmounted horses under control as Teodor and Witez took the lead. The entire caravan stretched for miles and Teodor was far enough back that the jeeps and trucks carrying the mares and foals were out of sight.

The journey to the border would take all day and into the next morning—if all went well. When night fell and the owls called out their warnings, the horses were placed in pre-selected pastures to rest and graze. The men and families found soft ground to settle down upon.

Teodor climbed over the fence that secured the pasture holding Witez and the stallions he was traveling with. Teodor could see the dark figure of his horse a short distance away. He watched him shuffle through the tall grass, searching for the best specimens. Satisfied that his horse was safe, he sat beside the fence and leaned against a post. He let his heavy eyes close.

Teodor awoke when the first sign of sunlight appeared in the east. He rubbed the sleep from his eyes and looked around. Beside him, Witez lay in the grass, his eyes closed, deep breaths rhythmically moving his chest. Teodor leaned over and pressed his body against the stallion's shoulder and rubbed his shiny, brown coat. Witez opened his eyes and let out a soft nicker of welcome.

Quinlivan was already up and supervising the loading of the mares and foals into the trucks. Stewart was distributing bread and coffee to the grooms and soldiers. Lessing was checking on each of the groups of horses. These horses were not accustomed to long treks, and most were not shod. The biggest issue the vet was facing was sore hooves.

With the return of Reed to the American post, Quinlivan was now the officer in charge. He was eager to get moving. The previous day had gone fairly smoothly, with the exception of a few encounters with small arms fire during which no injuries were sustained. He hoped today would be the same. They were heading toward Furth im Wald, just a few hours away. There, they planned to cross the Chamb River which separated Czechoslovakia and Germany.

Teodor headed down the road on Witez's back, calmly leading a large group of stallions. The other riders with his band of horses rode alongside the loose horses, doing their best to keep them from wandering off. Teodor rubbed Witez's neck as he looked around at the unfamiliar countryside. Large swaths of pastureland were intersected with clusters of deciduous and evergreen trees. The bright sun in the cloudless sky warmed his back. The group of horses ahead of him disappeared over the crest of a hill. Teodor directed Witez up the road as it snaked up the hill. He glanced back to make sure his stallions were following him. All seemed to be in order, and he smiled.

As he reached the top of the hill, Witez came to a sudden stop, lifted his head, and let out a loud snort. Teodor turned to face forward. His eyes opened wide, and his jaw dropped. He stood overlooking the little border town of Furth im Wald. Beyond the town of tall, narrow houses, the river Chamb worked its way through the valley like a wandering snake, feeding green pastures as it passed. A lovely, quaint stone bridge arched over the flowing waters of the swiftly moving river. On the far side of the bridge was the land they were seeking — Germany.

But it was not the beauty of the landscape that caught his attention. On this side of the bridge was a mass of trucks, jeeps, and loose horses. A red and white barrier was stretched across the entrance to the bridge, blocking passage. From this vantage point, it was difficult for Teodor to ascertain what was happening. But he was wise enough to know that it wasn't good.

He remained in place at the top of the hill as the rest of his group caught up with him. One of the other riders came up beside him. "What's wrong? Why have you stopped?"

Teodor pointed to the scene below.

The man, one of Prince Amassov's soldiers, turned his head. He mumbled a Russian swear word under his breath as he pulled out a pair of field glasses. Teodor looked down, his face blushing. Languages were easy for the boy, and he knew just what the soldier had said.

With the glasses pressed against his face, the Cossack soldier surveyed the situation. "We're in trouble," he said, still peering through the binoculars. "It appears there are three Czechoslovakian partisans, heavily armed, blocking our passage. Here, have a look," he said, handing the field glasses to Teodor.

Teodor took the glasses. He watched as Lieutenant Quinlivan rode up to the front of the line and stopped at the roadblock. He waved his arms and he appeared to be shouting at the guards. The guards responded by raising their weapons and pointing them at Quinlivan and Lessing.

Through the glasses, Teodor noticed a lone American soldier near the back of the line of trucks disappear into the forest on horseback. A few minutes later the soldier returned, followed by an M8 armored car that came rumbling through the trees, smashing the brush as it rolled along. It came to a halt in front of the trucks holding the mares and foals. The turret on the armored car swung forward, and the muzzle of its 37 mm gun took aim at the Czechs. Even from this distance, Teodor could feel the tension as the Czech partisans with their red communist armbands glared down the muzzle of the huge gun. Teodor held his breath.

"What's happening," his companion said. "Let me see."

Dropping the glasses from his eyes but continuing to stare at the scene below, Teodor handed him the binoculars.

"They raised the gates!" the Cossack exclaimed as he peered through the glasses. He passed the glasses back to Teodor. "Look for yourself," he said as Teodor took the binoculars.

Teodor watched as the Czech soldiers stepped away. Quinlivan and Lessing spurred their horses forward and trotted over the bridge. The horse vans and jeeps followed. Soon, the first group of horses began to cross.

"Teodor moving on," the boy said, giving Witez a nudge with his calves. With a whoop and a shout, the herdsmen in his group moved their stallions down the steep winding road leading to Furth im Wald.

Upon reaching the bottom of the hill and entering the village, Teodor did not look to the right or the left. He was keenly aware of the villagers lining the streets. But his eyes were locked on the arch of the stone bridge directly ahead. The last of the group of horses in front of him had crossed by the time Witez set a dainty hoof on the flat stones. With the clippity-clop sound that was music to Teodor's ears, Witez carried the two of them away from

the enslavement of the Nazis to what promised
to be a new life of freedom

PART 2

LIFE IN AMERICA

Chapter 26

Mansbach, May 1945

For eight long days, Teodor and Witez trudged along the roadways. At night, Teodor packed Witez's hooves with sticky mud, but even that didn't keep the stallion from getting footsore. Teodor marveled that Witez's kind, patient nature kept him going, even as his pace slowed and a slight limp appeared in his gate. But, unlike most of the horses, Witez's indomitable spirit seemed to thrive on the adventure.

The long, increasingly hot and humid days were followed by dark and lonely nights. This gave Teodor one thing, however, and that was plenty of time to think. He struggled to interpret the unique emotions he was experiencing. Fear of the unknown held a prominent place, but it was also accompanied by some degree of fascination with the newness of the world around him. The order imposed upon the members of the Army by Quinlivan and Stewart was comfortable for Teodor, and he thrived in the environment of contrived security.

Many times his thoughts centered on his mother. It made his heart hurt to think of the final embrace they shared . . . a level of physical closeness he usually denied himself. The exception, of course, being when it came to Witez. But Witez was different. Witez was a part of him and he a part of the stallion.

Teodor even had time to entertain fleeting thoughts of his father. He had to resist the urge to reach into his pocket and stroke a silver pin that was no longer there.

He struggled to connect with some of the other riders. It took all his strength and determination to stand near them during the occasional breaks or sparse meals. When he did sit down close to them, he was treated initially with kindness. The men tried talking to him about his home, about horses, about his plans. But as the men's attempts at conversation were met with silence or one or two words, they soon quit trying. This was fine with Teodor. He preferred to just sit and listen. He did not want to be the center of attention nor the topic of discussion.

Their final destination was a luxurious stud in Mansbach located near Munich that had been taken over by the Wehrmacht in 1933. It was now under the control of the Americans. The facility was so large, it could stable eight hundred horses. But they were facing a journey of about three hundred and twenty kilometers (two hundred miles) in order to reach it.

On the eighth day, Teodor and Witez dragged their tired bodies through the Stud's gates just as the sun was setting. The boy didn't think he had ever seen anything as beautiful as the rows of whitewashed stone buildings with red roofs. Teodor dropped to the cobblestones that covered the courtyard and led his horse to the first stall in the row. One by one, the stallions in his group were bedded down, fed, watered, and checked for injuries.

Once all the horses were cared for, most of the riders retreated to the little town to find a pub in which to quench their thirst. Since cots had not yet been set up or assigned, Teodor retired to the soft hay in Witez's stall. He was tired to the point of exhaustion but grateful to have Witez in a safe place.

Teodor woke to the sound of shouting voices.

"We have a mare ready to deliver. Where is Dr. Lessing?"

Teodor sprang to his feet. Witez, sleeping soundly, was startled awake. "Teodor be back," he whispered as he slid the stall door open. A light was shining at the end of the row of stalls, casting a golden beam across the aisleway. The rest of the barn was dark and quiet, the horses glad to settle in after their long journey. Teodor ran toward the light.

Two grooms were standing in the stall. A white Lipizzaner mare was on her side, breathing heavily. On occasion, she would lift her head and stare back at her distended belly before letting her head collapse back onto the straw.

"What should we do?" asked one groom, wiping sweat from his brow.

"Maybe we should try to pull it out," suggested the other.

Teodor put up his hand and shook his head. "Leave her alone," he said softly.

"Are you sure?" said the first.

Teodor, remembering the birth of the foal in Hostau, nodded.

As the swallows in the barn began leaving their nests and the silver light of dawn turned golden, Teodor and the grooms watched as the miracle of life came forth in this new land. To Teodor, it was a promise of a new life to come for him and Witez.

Chapter 27

Order and routine were quickly established in Mansbach. Several of the refugees moved on to find new lives for themselves. The POWs were thrilled to be released to their respective armed forces. While Prince Amassov and his Cossacks remained in Mansbach to help care for the horses, there were still far fewer grooms and riders to do all the work required. As a result, Teodor no longer cared only for Witez. He had several horses, all stallions, that he needed to feed, water, groom, and ride. But Teodor thrived in the daily schedule of work that remained the same day after day. He rarely had time to think of his mother or the life he left behind. At night he dropped onto his cot and spent each dreamless night sleeping soundly.

The unconditional surrender of the German Third Reich had been signed almost a month before, in the early morning hours of Monday, May 7, 1945. While the bloodshed largely ceased, there was a massive cleanup to do, not the least of which was determining what should become of the beautiful horses from Hostau. Two hundred and nineteen Lipizzaners from the Spanish Riding School in Vienna were claimed by the director of the famous school, Colonel Alois Podhajsky. They were easily identified by their brand. At last, Podhajsky's horses could return home to continue their tradition of developing the finest horses and riders in the world. He realized that without the efforts of the U.S. Army, his precious horses would have been lost forever.

The Spanish Riding School's Lipizzaners were sent on their way by train. Teodor watched them being loaded into the same makeshift trucks that brought them out of Czechoslovakia, to be transported to the train station. There they were loaded in warm cars with plenty of feed and deep straw for bedding. Teodor felt a sadness weigh heavily on his heart as he watched them being taken away. He would miss the magnificent animals. Yet he was grateful that they were going home at last.

He turned and went back to Witez's stall. "Where will Teodor and Witez go?" he whispered.

The answer to that question came shortly thereafter. Several other horses were claimed by their owners after proof of ownership was provided. Others were given to good homes in the area. In all, Colonel Reed staked claim to around a hundred of the Lipizzaners, Thoroughbreds, and Arabians, all of the finest quality. Witez was one of those.

After the war, Reed wanted to demonstrate to the Army that the horse could still play a viable role for the Army. He organized mounted patrols to weave through the thick forests that formed the border between Czechoslovakia and Bavaria. Teodor, being little more than a prisoner of war, was not sent on these patrols, and no one dared attempt to ride "Teodor's horse."

Then came the day in early June 1945 that Colonel Reed, Captain Stewart, and Colonel Rudofsky, who came from Hostau, were called to testify at the Third Army headquarters regarding the ownership of the remaining horses. The three men gave clear and convincing testimony that the horses were all lawful war prizes and the property of the US Government.

While this was happening, General Patton was in the States, meeting with the new head of the Army Remount Service, Colonel Fred Hamilton, to plead the case for preserving and protecting the horses. He claimed that the horses would be a great asset to the Army's own breeding program.

As a result of these two meetings, Colonel Hamilton paid a personal visit to the stables in Germany where the horses were housed, beginning with Mansbach.

One unusually bright June morning, Teodor was summoned by Quinlivan.

"Young man," Quinlivan began, "we have a very important visitor coming this morning. He will be selecting the horses to be kept by the United States Army and shipped to America. I would like Witez to be one of the horses selected. Please make sure he is perfectly groomed and ready for inspection."

Teodor nodded his assent and left Quinlivan's office. The boy could feel his heart pounding, and he twisted his sweating hands together as he hurried back to the stable where Witez was contentedly munching on his breakfast. It didn't take much to get Witez ready for this visitor, as Teodor always had the bay stallion looking immaculate. Teodor grabbed the tail comb and made sure Witez's mane and tail were tangle-free and any errant strands were in place. Taking a clean cloth, he wiped any unwanted specks of dust from his shining coat. He stepped back and examined his work. Pleased, he stepped up to Witez and cupped the soft muzzle in his hands. Looking into the deep brown eyes he said, "Today is the day, Witez. Today we find out if we become Americans."

He was struck with a sudden terrifying thought. *What if they don't pick Witez? Or worse, what if they take Witez and not me?*

Teodor shook his head and pressed his palms against his temples. He couldn't let that happen. He had to show them how valuable he was as Witez's groom and what a great horseman he was becoming.

Colonel Hamilton's first stop on his tour to the four main German Studs was Mansbach. He had heard much about the magnificent stallion, Witez II, and was eager to see if the rumors were true or just hyperbole born of war weariness. When Teodor walked the stallion out of the stables, Hamilton knew immediately that the tales had not been an exaggeration. Truly, this horse was a perfect specimen of what the Arabian horse should be like, from his small muzzle to his inward pointing ears, down the gracefully arched neck attached to the sloping shoulders leading down to the dainty hooves. It was hard for Hamilton to take his eyes off the animal.

Of course, this horse must go to America.

Chapter 28

After an idyllic summer of riding nearly every day, Teodor and Witez were strong and healthy. They spent long hours practicing in the Stud's arena or hacking through the peaceful countryside. The world had suddenly changed for horses and humans alike, and they were reveling in it.

Quinlivan often joined him, riding Lotnik. The magnificent, gray stallion was also from Witez's birthplace in Janow, Poland. Dr. Lessing came along on Indigo at least weekly. On rare occasions, even Colonel Reed visited the Stud to go for a ride, requesting Teodor to come with him as a guide. Teodor could not have been happier.

The leaves were just starting to change color and the air beginning to offer a hint of crispness when Teodor and Witez returned to the Stud from an early morning hack.

Quinlivan, now promoted to Captain with the departure of Colonel Reed and Captain Stewart, stood in the courtyard waiting for the boy to return. Beside him stood the two veterinarians, Lessing and Kroll.

Teodor dismounted and led Witez up to the men, stopping just in front of them. His eyes looked down at the ground.

"Teodor," began Quinlivan, "Colonel Hamilton has made his selection of the horses to be shipped to America." He paused and looked back and forth between the two vets and smiled. "Witez has been chosen as, of course, we knew he would be."

Teodor nodded, his eyes still looking at the ground; his hands twisting the reins connecting him to his horse.

Quinlivan continued. "I have been asked to accompany the horses on the ship that will carry them across the Atlantic. Colonel Reed asked both Dr. Lessing and Dr. Kroll to go as well. Because there is not room for Dr. Lessing's family, he has chosen not to come. Dr. Kroll, on the other hand, is eager to begin a new life in America."

Teodor felt his heart start to pound. His breathing became short and shallow.

Kroll stepped up to him. "Young man, I would like you to come along as my assistant."

Teodor whirled around and threw his arms around Witez's neck. His shoulders shook as he cried, his face buried in the stallion's mane.

"Is that a yes?" Kroll said with a chuckle.

"Y-yes," Teodor stuttered.

Chapter 29

Aboard the ship Stephen F. Austin, October 1945

Thus, another journey lay before the stallion Witez and his peculiar boy. The falling leaves seemed to suggest that Mansbach was weeping as it watched the horses being led onto trucks. Teodor held onto Witez's lead rope as he walked up the ramp. The stallion obediently followed. Once he was secured in the front of the truck, more stallions were brought in, with Lotnik placed right beside his Polish brother. Teodor hurried out of the truck and helped Quinlivan raise and secure the ramp. Walking around the side of the truck, Teodor found the white star on Witez's forehead shining though the slats. "Just a short ride, this time," he said to his horse before climbing into the cab.

The truck took them to the nearest train station, where Witez and the other horses were loaded aboard a special train bound for the port city of Bremerhaven. Teodor stayed with Witez in the train car, but the stallion, having been on a train when he was shipped from Janow to Hostau, was not the least bit bothered. Teodor stood beside him, rubbing his neck but realizing it wasn't really necessary. *Perhaps, I need Witez more than he needs me,* he thought as each click of the wheels and sway of the car took them farther and farther from home. As they moved north, Teodor's heart yearned for Hostau and, especially, for his mother.

The trip from Mansbach to Bremerhaven on the North Sea was over two hundred miles. During that time, Teodor made sure Witez had water and food and clean straw for bedding. The rumbling in Teodor's own stomach didn't bother him. He was too focused on caring for his horse.

They arrived in Bremerhaven on the morning of October 12. The day was cold and overcast. The air smelled of fish and tasted of salt. Enormous ships were lined up at the docks, waiting to be loaded with the large crates that seemed to be everywhere. The noise of machinery and shouting longshoremen was overwhelming and confusing to the boy. Teodor had never been anywhere like this. He covered his ears and ran back to the train car holding Witez. He dropped to the straw facing the corner of the stall. Sitting cross-legged, he closed his eyes. With his hands still covering his ears, he started rocking forward and back, forward and back. A deep groan arose from his belly and a quiver ran through his entire body. Witez moved through the straw and stopped in front of him. Dropping his head and letting his long mane fall forward, the horse provided the shelter from the world that Teodor needed.

Teodor dropped his hands and jerked open his eyes when he felt a firm hand grasp his shoulder. "You need to get a hold of yourself." A German voice Teodor recognized as Dr. Kroll rang in his ear. "I need your help right now. It's time to start loading the horses onto the ship."

Teodor took a deep breath, lifted his chin, and stood up. *I can do this for Witez,* he told himself.

The ship that was prepared for the horses was a several-year-old Liberty ship called the *Stephen F. Austin,* named for the man credited with settling Texas. On September 27, 1941, the United States launched the first of 2,700 Liberty class ships. Each ship was made up of 250,000 parts which were prefabricated throughout the country and welded together in about 70 days. Each liberty ship measured

441 feet tall and 56 feet at its beam or widest point and could sail at a top speed of eleven knots. They were the workhorses for the American Armed Forces, in some instances even adapted to be troop transports. Box stalls for the stallions, standing "tie" stalls for the mares, and small paddocks that could hold six to eight foals, were prepared for the precious cargo soon to come aboard.

When it was time to load the horses, Teodor led Witez into a narrow wooden crate which held him securely. The crate was lifted in the air with a crane and swung through the sky up and over the railing. Witez's eyes opened so wide, Teodor could see them ringed with white. But the stallion stood still and quiet. Teodor ran up the gangplank to meet his horse when he was lowered to the deck.

One by one, each horse was loaded on the ship in the same manner. At first it all went smoothly. The other Arabians and all the Thoroughbreds remained calm and well-behaved as they were loaded in the crate, lifted through the air, unloaded, and taken to their stalls.

Then it was time to load the Lipizzaners. Not only were most of the Lipizzaner mares that were born in Hostau untrained, but few of them were even halter-broken. Their lack of handling made it difficult to get them into a tight crate by themselves and the fear they felt being lifted in the air presented itself as whinnies, pawing and kicking.

Teodor viewed the process from the deck of the ship. Gripping the ship's railing, his heart raced as he watched one of the mares tossing her head and kicking at the sides. He feared she would break through the wooden sides of the box and fall to her death. Holding his breath, he clenched his teeth and kept his eyes on the mare. As soon as the crate was lowered to the deck, he put a rope around her neck. When the front of the crate was opened, she bolted out, dragging Teodor across the slick metal surface of the ship. Two other grooms threw out their arms and managed to stop the horse. Teodor stood and brushed himself off. His palms were red from rope burns. His elbows were rubbed raw and bleeding. But the mare was safe, and that was all that mattered to him.

With all the horses in their stalls, the loud blast of the ship's horn signaled the time to depart. Teodor ran to the back of the ship and watched as they pulled away from the dock, away from Germany. He turned and ran to the front. Standing on the bow, he stared at the sea to the west. Ahead was open water, taking him to a new land and a new life. He pursed his lips as tears stung the backs of his eyes. Slowly, his mouth lifted into a smile.

The trip across the ocean was supposed to take ten to twelve days. As a cautionary measure, hay and grain for twelve days was stocked on board. Lots of straw was also supplied to provide deep bedding. But a few days in on their journey, just as Teodor and Witez had adjusted to the constant rocking of the ship and had their "sea legs" as it is said, disaster struck.

Teodor decided to take a much-needed break from tending to the horses. He climbed the steep metal stairs that led to the deck. Stepping out the door at the top of the stairs, he was immediately greeted with a shower of sea spray. He held to the railing as he worked his way to the starboard side of the ship. He gazed to the west. Ahead, he saw a solid bank of black clouds that covered the horizon as far as he could see. As he stood gazing at the gray waters, the wind picked up and the waves grew in size and ferocity. Whitecaps appeared at the tops of the waves. They curled over and slapped the sides of the ship. Suddenly, a bolt of lightning shimmied across the water. The clap of thunder that followed seemed to land right on top of Teodor. Covering his ears, he ran back to the door. Struggling against the wind that pushed back against the door and wanted to keep it shut, he was finally able to open it enough to squeeze through. As he stepped in, the door slammed shut behind him. He rushed down the stairs, holding to the side rails. Bouncing from side to side, he found his way to Witez's stall. Slipping inside, he collapsed on the straw and covered his ears. Witez bent his neck down and nuzzled his head.

The ship sailed into a violent storm. The ship's cargo, being mostly animals and a few humans, was much lighter on the water than she was built for. As a result, the *Stephen F. Austin* was tossed from wave to giant wave. The foals in the pens were bounced off their feet. Many were stepped on by the other foals. The sailors did their best to hold onto the little ones as the ship forcefully rolled back and forth. The larger horses managed to brace themselves in their deep straw fairly well. One mare fell against the sides of her stall so hard that the wall broke, sending her crashing into the mare next to her.

"Teodor, come help!" Quinlivan called.

Teodor opened his eyes, took his hands from his ears, and pushed up. He fell against Witez's shoulder as he struggled to get to the stall door. Once out of the stall, he worked his way down the aisleway, getting knocked from side to side. He reached the collapsed stall and used all his strength to help the two horses while avoiding getting kicked by the flailing hooves. It took several men to pull them to safety from beneath the splintered wood. Once the horses were on their feet, Teodor held their shanks while Quinlivan and Kroll managed to reassemble the stall.

But the storm raged on . . . and on.

After several days, the ship's captain decided to turn south in hopes of finding smoother seas. While this proved to be successful, it created another problem. The detour added several days to the length of the journey. They didn't have enough food to last the additional days and the hay began to run short. Rather than stop to resupply in The Azores, it was decided to mix some of the straw in with the hay for added roughage and head directly for the States.

That proved to be a mistake.

Teodor fell into a deep sleep as soon as his head hit the small, hard pillow on his bunk. Sometime in the darkest part of the night, he was shaken awake. "Teodor, get up. We've got trouble," Kroll said in the darkness.

Teodor threw back his thin, wool blanket and dropped to the ship's floor. He pulled on his pants and as he shoved his arms in his shirt he said, "What is it? A mare delivering?"

"I only wish," responded Kroll. "We have a berth full of colicing horses. It appears all one hundred and fifty of them have a bad bellyache."

"Witez?"

"'Fraid so."

Teodor started running.

Every available groom and sailor was called into action. The worst cases had to have a tube inserted down their throats to their bellies. A mixture of oil and ether provided the necessary cure. The men found convincing a thrashing, untrained mare, or a strong-willed stallion that this would be good for them was a tough job.

The horses with milder symptoms, which included Witez, were haltered and led up and down the aisles between the stalls. Teodor haltered both Witez and Lotnik, clipped a lead rope on each, and spent the next three hours walking them. He didn't quit until each horse had passed a healthy pile of manure.

Just when they thought they had every horse on the mend, a non-equestrian sailor ran up to Dr. Kroll and Teodor as they were making their final rounds of all the stalls. "Dr.

Kroll, come quick. Another horse is colicing!" the sailor said.

Kroll and Teodor ran down the aisle past the stallion stalls to the row of mares, stopping at the stall at which the sailor was pointing. The mare was clearly in distress. "Bring her out," Kroll shouted at Teodor. The young teen stepped into the stall, untied the mare, and backed her out.

"Do you need me to get the tube?" Teodor asked.

Kroll smiled. "Not for this one. We'll even let her lie down."

Less than half an hour later, Teodor was rubbing a new foal dry with fresh straw.

Kroll stood beside him, his hands on his hips and a piece of straw hanging from his mouth. "Colic and labor can look a lot alike," he said, pleased with the results of a long night's work.

The *Stephen F. Austin* had left Bremerhaven with 151 horses but would be arriving in America with 152!

Chapter 30

Front Royal, April 7, 1946

The entire journey across the Atlantic lasted twenty-one days. When at last the *Stephen F. Austin* came into port at Newport News, Virginia, it was a tired and hungry cargo of horses and humans that disembarked. Having run out of feed two days before, the horses were weak and thin. Their coats and eyes were dull. Even the nursing foals had depleted their mothers' supply of milk. If the trip had taken any longer, several of the horses undoubtedly would have been lost.

Colonel Hamilton met the ship and immediately sent the horses on their way to the Aleshire Army Remount Depot in Front Royal, Virginia. For several months the horses were kept out of the public eye as they were brought back to health and full strength. Hidden away, Teodor and Witez were oblivious to the verbal conflict going on outside the stable. Some people complained that the horses took up valuable berths that could have been used to bring their sons home sooner. Others resisted the very idea of mixing German horse blood with American horse blood. But horsemen all around the country couldn't quell their curiosity about the captured horses. Keeping them hidden only heightened the anticipation of one day seeing them.

On April 7, 1946, Quinlivan shared his pride and joy with the world. A special public viewing parade was organized in the outdoor arena at Front Royal. That morning, Quinlivan walked through the stables, rubbing faces and passing out sugar cubes to the animals he deemed his friends. He stopped at Witez's stall.

"Teodor," he said. "How are you and your horse doing?"

Teodor looked down and smiled. He nodded his head to signify that all was well.

Quinlivan rubbed Witez's white star on his forehead. "Witez looks in fine shape. Has he been working well?"

"Yes, sir," Teodor whispered.

"Good. Good. Glad to hear it."

At two in the afternoon, the parade of horses began. A hush fell over the full-to-overflowing bleachers as, one by one, the horses captured from the Nazis were led around the arena. Teodor waited in the stable until the Arabians were lined up. Witez was to be the last.

As Teodor stepped out of the stable, he squinted in the bright sunshine. He could barely make out all the people in the stands. But Witez could see them. He lifted his head and snorted; his ears pricked forward. Arching his neck, he lifted his tail and pranced beside Teodor.

"Show-off," whispered Teodor, but he couldn't help but smile.

Quinlivan watched and listened as the whispers of approval flowed through the crowd. He hoped Witez and the other horses would have the power to help him keep the Army's horse program going. Thus, even with all their admirers, these horses were not for sale. His plan was to disperse the horses among the Army's six major horse-breeding facilities across the country.

Chapter 31

Pomona, California, Summer 1946

A few weeks later, Witez and Teodor were put on a train with the other Arabians and some of the Lipizzaners and traveled across the vast American continent, ending their journey in Pomona, California. It was, thankfully, an uneventful trip. Teodor thrilled at the scenery as they passed from state to state. Tree-covered mountains flattened and were replaced by rolling hills of grain. Wide open spaces of cattle range changed in an instant to the wild and rugged Rocky Mountains. Deserts with their strange flora and fauna were replaced by more mountains and, at last, fertile valleys.

Teodor stood beside Witez's head as they watched through the narrow gaps in the train car as the countryside skimmed by. The stallion's ears twitched back and forth as his boy pointed out one interesting sight after another. It seemed he was understanding everything Teodor was saying. "Look at the size of that river! Look at that deep canyon! Just imagine that jagged peak covered with snow!" Teodor was having the time of his life. Witez seemed to patiently take it all in.

When they arrived at the Kellogg Ranch in Pomona, outside Los Angeles, Teodor was sure they had found paradise.

The Army had been gifted the fabulous facility at the base of the San Gabriel Mountains in a roundabout manner. The nearly four-hundred-acre ranch was first purchased by W.K. Kellogg, the breakfast cereal magnate, in 1925. His intent was to create a world-class Arabian horse breeding facility. After years of investing in his dream, Kellogg succeeded in building a showplace, and he became a world-famous breeder of purebred Arabians. The ranch became a tourist attraction as well, drawing hundreds of guests to its Sunday horse shows. Almost one hundred purebred Arabians called the Kellogg ranch their home by the time Kellogg donated the ranch and the horses to the University of California in 1932 so that the school could create an institute of horse husbandry. The ceremony surrounding the donation was equally spectacular, with the famous humorist Will Rogers functioning as the emcee.

Once World War II broke out, Kellogg encouraged the University to donate his ranch to the Army as a way of supporting the war effort. The school did so. However, by this time, the Army had already begun dismounting its troops. The Kellogg ranch never supplied any horses for the war.

By the time Witez arrived, the ranch was one of the premier Arabian breeding facilities in the world. The Army immediately began offering Witez as a stud, a task for which he was very successful. Colonel F.W. Koester, the new head of the Army Remount station in Pomona, was a fighting advocate for the horses. And fight he must. In order to ensure the value of the Arabians, he had to get them registered with the American Breeding Associations, which were skeptical of the authenticity of their bloodlines. With the help of Captain Quinlivan, he was able to do so. Through their joint efforts, both Witez and Lotnik were finally registered with the Arabian Horse Registry of America.

But storm clouds continued to roll over all the horses brought over the ocean on that rough journey. The animals, including Witez, were frequently in the news. Several European countries, including Poland, sued the U.S. Government over ownership of the horses.

After much debate, the Senate Armed Services committee ruled that the rescued equines were legitimate spoils of war.

It was a happy day for Teodor when he heard the news.

"Teodor," called Colonel Koester from the end of the long aisleway that ran in front of the stalls.

Teodor leaned out the open top half of Witez's stall door.

"Great news, Teodor," Koester said, hustling up to the stall. "Witez is now officially a U.S. Citizen, and I have submitted the paperwork that will begin the process to make you a citizen along with him!"

Teodor whirled around to face his stallion.

"Did you hear that, Witez? We are home now. We're not going anywhere."

Chapter 32

Kellogg Ranch, Fall 1948

Teodor was warming up Witez in the covered arena in preparation for the weekly Sunday show. Visitors were already streaming in and finding their seats. People were visiting and laughing in the warm November sunshine. But one couple was standing off to the side by themselves, watching Teodor as he rode Witez. The man, in his late forties, was tall and fit. His tanned, clean-shaven face was shaded by his cream-colored Stetson. The woman beside him was only slightly shorter, but several years younger and equally trim. The tight curls that covered her head were light brown, and her eyes were kind. She smiled as she watched Teodor and Witez.

Teodor noticed them but didn't stop to greet them.

In the more than two years that Teodor and Witez had called Pomona their home, the young boy was becoming a man and the horse a mature, muscled stallion. The two of them had a partnership that could be rivaled only by the best horsemen and horses in the world. Riding Witez was the greatest joy in Teodor's life, and it gave him the confidence to face the unknowns in an uncertain world. Teodor knew he had changed. While he still had trouble looking people in the eye, he found he could converse with them confidently, especially if the subject was horses, which in this environment, it always was. He liked his changes. He liked himself. He liked his life.

As Teodor finished his workout with Witez, he slowed the horse to a walk and dismounted. Leading the stallion to the gate, he opened it and stepped through. As he did so, the couple who had been watching him ride stepped up to him.

"Hello, young man," said the man. "You are an excellent rider."

Teodor blushed. "Thank you, but I must give Witez the credit for making me look good," he said in a thick Eastern European accent.

The woman stepped up and ran her white gloved hand over Witez's neck. "He is such a lovely horse."

"Yes. He is the best there is," said Teodor.

"Is he as kind as he seems?" she asked.

"Oh, yes. He never gives me the least bit of trouble. I can't say the same for all the stallions."

The couple both chuckled. "Yes. We know what you mean," said the man. "My name is Mr. Earle E. Hurlbutt, and this is my wife, Mrs. Frances Hurlbutt. We own the Calarabia Ranch near Calabasas."

"It is nice to meet you," Teodor said without extending his hand.

"If Witez was not owned by the Army, I would do anything to add him to my herd," said Mr. Hurlbutt. "But since that is not possible, I have decided to do the next best thing. I will be sending my best mare to him so that I can at least have one of his sons or daughters."

Times change and opportunities present themselves seemingly out of nowhere. While Witez was winning admirers in California, the powers-that-be in Washington DC were making plans that would change his life again. On July 1, 1948, the Army removed horses from its programs and turned the remount stations over to the Department of Agriculture. To the bureaucrats in that department, the horses and breeding facilities were nothing but a drain on their budget. Horses were being phased out of the Army at an alarming rate. In 1941 there were 200,000 horses in their ranks. By 1949, the plan was to have only 327. So, all but the remount station in Reno, Oklahoma, had to go. Pomona was the first to hit the chopping block. Teodor's only consolation was that Witez would not be auctioned off . . . yet. He was to be shipped to Oklahoma.

At the time of its closure, the Kellogg ranch was home to 175 Arabians. A few mares were given to the University of Washington and a few more to the University of Idaho. A few dozen horses were sent to Oklahoma and the rest, 125 stallions, mares, and foals were to be auctioned off on December 17, 1948.

In addition to selling off the horses, the entire ranch and all the equipment was to be declared surplus and would be disposed of.

The local people were up in arms. Whether a horse aficionado or not, the citizens were proud of the world-famous Arabian ranch. President Truman received appeals in both letter form and in person. Even an ambitious, young congressman by the name of Richard Nixon sent an appeal to the Agriculture Department. It was hoped that the ranch and the horses could remain intact under new ownership.

Their attempts failed.

And thus, with a final sugar lump from Colonel Koester and a pat on the back for Teodor, the stallion and his peculiar boy boarded a train for the journey to Oklahoma. With a heavy heart, Teodor and Witez looked out the slats of the rail car and watched their beautiful home slip into the distance. The train rattled east carrying with it one of the most beautiful horses the world ever produced.

Chapter 33

Fort Reno, Oklahoma, Spring 1949

Oklahoma was a pleasant enough place. Not as fancy as the Kellogg Ranch, but there was plenty of good feed and lots of open space to ride across. The winter was cold and dreary by California standards, so Teodor kept Witez under a warm blanket when he was not riding him. He kept his water fresh, breaking the ice in the bucket most mornings. Each day Teodor fluffed up the straw bedding and added more just for good measure.

Spring came with warmer temperatures and sprigs of fresh green grass. Teodor kept busy caring for Witez and many of the other stallions. The staff at the Stud appreciated the talent the peculiar boy displayed caring for even the most difficult stallion. They all recognized the bond between Witez and the young man, and no one attempted to interfere.

Two grooms watched him closely. "The kid don't say much, but he sure knows how to work."

"I noticed he says a lot to that horse o' his. He speaks in a funny language, too."

"I heard he came over with the horses after the war. He's from somewhere in Eastern Europe, I think."

"You seen him ride? He can handle a western saddle as well as you. And I wager you'd fall right off the little English saddle he uses most of the time."

"Mighty fancy horse he has there. All these Arabs are pretty nice, but that's the cream o' the crop."

The two men went back to their tasks, but similar conversations were repeated often at Fort Reno.

Witez, now eleven, was in his prime. His muscles bulged under a sleek brown coat. His shimmering, black mane and tail flowed in the ubiquitous wind that whipped across the Oklahoma prairies.

But just as Teodor thought they had found a new home in which they could be comfortable, decisions were made far away in the nation's capital that would upend them again.

"Teodor," said the stablemaster on what would have otherwise been a beautiful day in May. "I'm sorry to tell you this, but the Department of Agriculture has decided to sell off the rest of the horses."

Teodor's mouth fell open and his knees buckled under him. He fell to the ground at Witez's feet.

"I know this comes as a shock to you. To all of us, actually. But it is out of our hands."

"When?" Teodor managed to squeak out.

"The auction is to be held on May 25th."

One week. Teodor had one week. His mind was a whirlwind of thoughts. Should he get on Witez and run away? Should he hide Witez with the local Indian tribe? Should he cover him with mud so no one would want him?

Then an idea struck him. An idea that just might work. Earle Hurlbutt. He needed to reach Earle Hurlbutt.

Florence and Earle Hurlbutt were enjoying a cup of tea on their veranda as they watched the new foals prance around the pasture just beyond the fence line. The trusty German Shepherd at their feet lifted his head and started barking as he ran to the front door.

"Someone's at the door, dear," said Mrs. Hurlbutt. "Would you mind getting it?"

"Of course. I'll be right back," Hurlbutt said as he placed his teacup in the saucer on the wrought iron table.

Hurlbutt walked toward the front door. He could see the shadow of a man through the side glass. Grabbing the dog's collar, he opened the door. Standing on the stoop was a Western Union delivery man.

"Mr. Hurlbutt?" the man asked.

"Yes. I am he."

"I have a telegram for you." The man stretched forth his hand in which he held a yellow and brown paper.

Hurlbutt took it from him, unfolded it, and started reading. When he looked up, his eyes were sparkling. "Thank you. Thank you, very much!"

The delivery man tipped his hat and said, "I'm glad it is good news. We don't always get to deliver good news."

Hurlbutt shut the door, let go of the dog, and ran to the veranda.

"Florence! Florence! It's a message from Teodor in Oklahoma. Witez is to be auctioned off in three days!"

"Witez?" She stood and threw her arms around her husband. "You must go."

"But can we afford him? It has been a tight year for us. And we haven't sold any of our foals yet."

Brushing his concerns aside with a wave of her hand, she said, "We must. We must find a way."

Hurlbutt and his wife stared toward the paddock in which a majestic chestnut stallion stood watching them. Just a yearling, Witez's son, Zitez, displayed all the qualities of his sire, just as the Hurlbutts had hoped. Now they felt their dream of owning Witez was within reach. Could it possibly be a dream come true for them?

They spent the next several hours going over their books and finding every spare penny that they could possibly do without. When all was said and done, Earle went to the bank and withdrew the large sum of $8,000.

The post-war air travel business, still in its infancy, was both expensive and inconvenient. Flights were sporadic. The best they could do was purchase a ticket on a flight from Los Angeles to Oklahoma City, then hire a driver to take him the twenty-five miles to Reno. While Hurlbutt struggled to make flight reservations, Florence packed him a suitcase. She drove him to the airport the next day. As she kissed him goodbye at the gate, she stuffed several fives, tens, and a couple of twenties in his pocket. In all, she gave him an extra $100. "From the Christmas jar," she said with a wink. "Don't leave him behind. He is meant to be with us."

Chapter 34

Fort Reno, Oklahoma, May 25, 1949

In one of the paddocks behind the grandstand, Teodor stood beside Witez. His horse, with the white star on his face and the number 131 painted on his croup, seemed oblivious to what was going on. Teodor felt his heart pounding, and Witez responded to his best friend's anxiety by rubbing his face against the boy's shoulder.

"Teodor," he heard someone call from over the fence.

Teodor turned. Standing by the fence, one booted foot resting on the bottom rail was Captain Stewart. Witez greeted the man with his deep whinny.

Teodor grinned and suddenly his heart was filled with hope. "Captain Stewart. I'm so glad to see you. Have you come to buy Witez?"

"I'm not Captain Stewart anymore. Just plain old Tom," he said as he reached over the fence, ruffled Teodor's hair, and stroked Witez's face. "You've done a mighty fine job of taking care of our boy."

"He's better than ever. You should see him. You're going to buy him, aren't you?"

Stewart pressed his lips together before shaking his head. "Oh, don't I wish I could. I haven't quite settled into life after the war, yet." Teodor looked into Stewart's eyes just long enough to catch the sadness there. "I came to say goodbye to my old friend."

Teodor dropped his chin to his chest.

"Don't worry, Teodor. Witez always comes out on top. He'll find a good home."

"Teodor's horse," the boy said firmly.

"Yes. He'll always be Teodor's horse."

The cab dropped Hurlbutt off at the dusty drive leading into the Army Remount near Reno, Oklahoma. Dressed in his nicest suit, the man from California walked between the wire fences toward the grandstand. He placed his hand over his suit pocket to reassure himself that his $8,000 in cash was still there. He found a seat in the middle of the fifth row and sat down. The auction had already begun, selling the Thoroughbreds first. An offspring of Man-o-War brought over a thousand dollars.

In the bleachers, Hurlbutt fidgeted in his seat. Craning his neck, he tried to see Witez. All the Thoroughbreds had now been shown and purchased. Now it was time for the Arabians. Hurlbutt's heart stopped, and he sucked in a quick breath. Standing at the gate was Witez looking like the prince he was. His dark eyes took in the crowd as a stunned silence filled the grandstand.

Teodor hesitated. His mind was racing. Was there any way to avoid this? He tried sending a telegram to the Hurlbutts but had not heard back from them. He felt like he was leading his horse and himself to their deaths. His feet felt like they were buried in cement. He couldn't move.

The announcer called out Witez's number. "Our next horse, Witez II, is an exotic Polish Arabian out of the famous Ofir. He is the jewel of the auction, and I am starting the bidding at $1,000. Would the groom please bring him into the arena?"

Teodor lowered his chin. "I guess we have to do this, Witez," he said. Witez nudged his shoulder, and Teodor reached over and rubbed his face. Then the boy raised his chin and, using all his strength, lifted a foot and stepped onto the sandy surface of the arena.

The moment Hurlbutt saw Witez step into the arena his heart started pounding. The stallion was magnificent. He had truly reached his acme. Hurlbutt knew it, but so did everyone else, and the bidding started with a flurry. It was up to $4,000 dollars before Hurlbutt had raised his number. He removed his brown wool fedora and wiped his brow before raising the bid to $4,100. But the bidding went up. At $5,000 he raised it to $5,100.

By the time it reached $6000, he was confident that $6100 would win the stallion. He was wrong. The bidding had slowed down, but it was still inching upward. Once it passed $7,000, he began to get nervous. He removed his handkerchief with a shaking hand and wiped his brow again. This time he also wiped the back of his neck. He was getting dangerously close to the $8,000 he had in his pocket.

"Seventy-five hundred," he shouted.

The people around him gasped as they stared at the man who was obviously so desperate to buy this horse. Beautiful as he was, that was hard for most of them to understand. The cattle ranchers were happy to buy a sturdy dependable quarter horse for a few hundred dollars. The movie producers knew there were more Arabians coming for their films set in Egypt. Even the circus people, living on tighter budgets, were willing to see what else the auction had to offer in terms of intelligent Arabians to train for their acts.

But someone else in the crowd wanted Witez as much as Hurlbutt.

"Seventy-six hundred."

Hurlbutt nearly threw his card in the air. "Seventy-seven hundred."

"Seventy-eight hundred."

Hurlbutt sucked in a deep breath. The people around him were holding theirs. One old cowboy patted him on the back. "Come on, buddy. You've gone this far. Might as well finish it."

Hurlbutt lifted his chin. "Seventy-nine hundred."

The people around him cheered.

Then, over the cheers, Hurlbutt heard, "Eight thousand."

His heart sank as his chin dropped. He turned, picked up his hat from his seat, and started to sit back down. As he did so, his hand brushed his pocket where a wad of Christmas money still remained. His wife's words echoed in his brain. "Don't leave him behind. He is meant to be with us."

Slowly, Hurlbutt stood, raised his number, and shouted, "EIGHT THOUSAND ONE HUNDRED!"

That was it. That was all there was. He couldn't bear to hear another bid. He couldn't bear to see his horse being handed over to someone else. He turned and started to walk away. Then, over the cheering crowds, he heard the announcer say, "Sold for $8,100 to the man in the brown fedora."

Chapter 35

Calarabia Ranch, June 1949

The June sun was soft over the San Fernando Valley as the train came to a stop at the station. Earle and Frances Hurlbutt had been sitting in the cab of their truck, eagerly awaiting the train's arrival for over an hour. Today was the day Witez II and his groom, Teodor, would join their family at the Calarabia Ranch.

The black smoke from the engine settled over the railcars as Frances and Earle climbed out of their truck with a horse trailer attached. They shielded their eyes from the sun as they peered down the line. "Which car?" Frances asked.

"I don't know. We'll just have to wait and see," her husband responded.

"I don't think I can wait another minute!"

Earle put his arm around her. "How do you feel about adding Teodor to our family?"

"I have always wanted a child; I just didn't know he would be nearly a grown man by the time we got a son."

"I don't think he'll need much mothering."

"No. I'm sure that's true, with what the boy has been through. I hope he'll be happy with us."

"I think he is happy anywhere Witez is."

The scraping sound of metal on metal reverberated down the platform as the door on one of the box cars slid open. A ramp was slid out and angled to the ground. Then a majestic brown head with a dished nose and a white star appeared in the opening. Beside him, holding the lead rope was a tall, thin, curly-haired young man.

The horse sniffed the air as he looked from side to side. The boy looked only at the horse. "We're home at last," he said.

Witez stepped delicately down the ramp behind Teodor. Once on the platform, they turned toward the couple who were hurrying toward them, wide smiles on their faces.

Stopping in front of the newest member of their Arabian family, Florence wiped a tear from her eye. She pulled a sugar cube from her purse and offered it to Witez who took it with soft, gentle lips.

Teodor said nothing but offered the shank to Mr. Hurlbutt. "No, no. You're his groom. You take him to the trailer," Hurlbutt said with a smile.

A short time later, Witez's new family was sitting in the pickup as it pulled the horse trailer toward Calarabia Ranch. Mrs. Hurlbutt sat between her husband and the boy.

"Teodor, I want you to know that we consider you as much a part of our family as we do Witez. You will always have a home at Calarabia for as long as you desire."

Teodor nodded his appreciation. "Thank you," he said, without looking up.

"I have prepared a room for you in the main house. I hope you will like it," she said.

"I will," he said.

"And we are fixing a special dinner for tonight. Do you like barbequed chicken?" she said with a smile.

"Yes. Thank you."

Mrs. Hurlbutt looked at her husband. "Earle, is there anything you'd like to tell Teodor," she said, elbowing him in the ribs.

"Ouch. Oh, yes. We are very glad to have you here." Then he leaned forward and winked at Teodor. "And don't mind Mrs. Hurlbutt. She always talks a blue streak." He leaned forward and switched on the radio.

The truck and trailer made a sharp turn off the main road and onto the drive leading to the lovely ranch. The home was a white, clapboard ranch-style home, nestled against the foothills. The large, white stable was behind the house. A few trees dotted the barnyard. Paddocks lined both sides of the drive. The mares and foals reacted to the arrival of the truck and trailer by running and bucking along the fence line. Witez whinnied a greeting, announcing his arrival to all, as if to say, "The Chieftain has arrived."

After backing Witez out of the trailer, Mrs. Hurlbutt, Mr. Hurlbutt, and Teodor led Witez to his new stall. On the door was a shiny new brass sign that said: *Witez II #3933, showing he was certified by the Arabian Horse Club. The asterisk before his name indicated that he was imported. The stall opened out to a large pasture, giving him the freedom to come and go as he pleased. Teodor put him in the stall, unclipped his halter, and stepped back. "Go ahead, Witez. It's all yours."

The stallion looked back and forth between Teodor and the open door. He turned away from the boy and slowly walked to the opposite side of the stall and looked out. The great outdoors awaited him. With one last look at Teodor, he let out a snort and bolted out the door. With head up and mane and tail flying behind him, the stallion galloped and bucked as he raced around the field.

Teodor and the Hurlbutts watched, their eyes shimmering with tears. Witez was home, and he knew it.

Chapter 36

Pomona Arabian Show, Fall 1951

Witez and Teodor couldn't have been happier in their new home. But the Hurlbutt's plans to use Witez as a stud to strengthen the American Arabian horse were slow to take hold. To be sure, a few mares were brought to him initially, but it wasn't until their offspring started winning in the breed classes at shows that people began to take notice.

Some, mainly those whose horses lost to the Witez foals, resisted this "newcomer" with his Polish bloodlines. The rumor was noised about that the youngsters wouldn't hold up in the long run. "Why else isn't Hurlbutt showing his stud?" many asked.

For Hurlbutt's part, he didn't feel he needed to waste time and money on the show ring. Anyone who saw his horse was immediately put under the stallion's spell. Still, the rumors persisted. "Obviously, Hurlbutt has something to hide," his competition insisted.

One night around the dinner table, Earle was late arriving. When he did join Frances and Teodor, he stomped in and jerked his chair back before sitting. His face was red, and his jaw was set, making his handsome features look hard.

Both Frances and Teodor stopped eating and stared at him.

"Earle, dear, whatever is the matter?" asked Mrs. Hurlbutt.

"Some horse people don't deserve to have horses!"

Teodor and Francis looked back and forth at one another.

"Yes, that's true, dear. Now please eat your dinner before it gets cold."

Earle grumbled under his breath as he snatched up his napkin and threw it in his lap. "All people need to do is come see him. Then they'll know for themselves that what they've heard is all a bunch of hogwash."

Teodor looked down and twisted his fork in his mashed potatoes.

Francis patted her husband's hand. "Don't listen to them. Witez is perfection. You know that. Teodor knows that. I know that. Isn't that what matters most?"

The next night the Hurlbutts were joined by Dean and Noy Christofferson, two brothers who were Arabian breeders from Lehi, Utah. They were returning from cleaning up the ribbons at the Pomona Arabian horse show. Their horse, and pride and joy, was a son of Witez named Yatez.

After paying their respects to their stallion's sire, they sat down for dinner with Earle, Francis, and Teodor. Small talk was soon replaced with a more serious discussion.

Noy, a tall, muscular man, turned to Earle. "Earle, it's time to show Witez."

"I don't need ribbons to know what a great horse he is."

"You know that, and Dean and I know that, but the rest of the Arabian show world is skeptical. And that skepticism is hurting his offspring. I'm having trouble getting mares to breed."

Dean jumped in. "They think you have something to hide."

"They're nothing but sore losers," grumbled Earle.

Noy threw up his hands. "You won't get any arguments from me. But I'm trying to run a breeding business and I'm just telling you how it is. If you would show Witez, it would help us a lot."

"Come on, Earle," added Dean. "Prove Witez's detractors wrong."

That fall, Witez was entered in the stallion class at the Southern California all-Arabian show in Pomona, the largest show at the time.

Mrs. Hurlbutt and Teodor were excited. Mr. Hurlbutt was grouchy. But, together, the three of them bathed and brushed, curried and combed, until Witez's coat shone like a copper penny and his mane and tail sparkled like the blackest obsidian.

It was a large class with many magnificent stallions ready to show their stuff. At thirteen, Witez was the oldest. The tension and excitement in the crowd was palpable. Teodor held onto Witez's lead rope, twisting it into a tighter and tighter circle as he watched the stallion before them go through his paces. His handler was an experienced showman. Teodor had had one week of instruction on breed showmanship. He had never been in a real ring with a real judge, at a real show, with real people watching!

When their number was called by the ring steward, Teodor took a deep breath and led Witez through his paces in front of the judges.

He blocked out all the noise and confusion around him and focused only on Witez. When at last they stopped in front of the judges, Teodor realized he had been holding his breath the whole time. He sucked in and let out a deep breath. Witez watched him then did the same. Teodor walked the length of the lead rope away from Witez, hoping that the horse would remember what they had worked on the past week. The horse stayed perfectly still, posing alertly like a statue. His ears pointing forward, his tail lifted. His eyes focused only on Teodor.

While Teodor and Witez were in the ring, Mr. and Mrs. Hurlbutt were watching from the stands. Frances was twisting her handkerchief in her lap. Earle was tapping the rolled-up program on his leg. The talk around them was about the newcomer whose name was not in the program.

Back in the arena, the judge was walking slowly around Witez. He looked at every leg, every muscle. Teodor felt his heart in his throat. He clenched his jaw and waited, almost challenging the judge to find a flaw.

The judge instructed Teodor to walk Witez away and trot back. The Hurlbutts in the stands weren't the only ones to ooh and aah at the sight. The horse was a symphony in motion.

Muscles rippled. Legs extended. Hocks and knees bending sharply. Seemingly as light as a feather, the horse floated across the ground as he trotted beside Teodor.

Back in place, at the end of the line, Teodor and Witez waited. In the stands, every breath was held. The judge took his time. At last, he handed his card to the announcer. "In first place, the winning stallion is Witez II owned by Earle and Frances Hurlbutt of..." the rest of the announcement was drowned out by the cheering. Witez had won.

The Stallion went on to compete against all the winners of the stallion classes, coming out on top again. Then he faced off against the champion mare. When Teodor led Witez from the ring, the Grand Champion rosette fluttered from the side of his halter. Witez had proven himself. Witez had forever silenced his detractors.

Chapter 37

The success in the show ring was repeated over and over again. The crowning honor came on a crisp fall day in October of 1953 when Witez was awarded the highest honor the Arabian Show world could give. He was presented with the trophy for the Pacific Coast Champion. At fifteen, he was the oldest stallion to ever receive this highest of honors.

Adding to the excitement for the Hurlbutts, with a promise of great things to come in the future, Witez's son, Zitez, was reserve champion.

"That's it," said Earle Hurlbutt as they drove home from the show with Witez in the trailer. "There is nothing more to prove."

"Witez can retire from the show ring knowing no one could beat him," added an almost giddy Frances Hurlbutt.

Teodor stared out the window at the passing orange and walnut orchards, a smile on his face.

"What's next for our boy?" asked Frances.

This question brought Teodor back to the conversation and he looked around Frances to study Earle's face.

The man was smiling. "We're going to spend all our time lining up the mares waiting to be bred!"

For the next seven years, Teodor and Witez hacked around the ranch, performed for visitors, and scheduled breeding sessions with the finest Arabian mares in the West. Hurlbutt's dream of strengthening the American Arabian horse was coming true.

One day, while Frances was sitting in the den thumbing through a magazine, she stumbled across an article from 1943 written by a man named Leo Kanner. He described eleven patients who displayed the same types of behaviors as she often saw in Teodor. One was a resistance to unexpected change. Another symptom was a need for order and an obsession with patterns. Also common was a difficulty with social interactions. The author of the article called it "Infantile Autism." As she kept searching, she found that the same doctor had written again in 1949 about this behavioral disorder he called "Autism" and concluded the cause was "Refrigerator Mothers," or parents who were cold and detached.

"Earle," Frances said one evening while Teodor was in the barn doing night check. "I have been reading about a disorder called 'Autism.' It sounds just like Teodor."

"Hmmm," Earle said from behind his *Arabian World* magazine.

"Earle, are you listening to me?"

Earle lowered his magazine. "Of course, dear. A disorder."

"Yes. The symptoms sound just like Teodor. But something is bothering me. This doctor believes the cause is cold or detached mothers. From what little I know about his mother, she was anything but cold and detached."

Earle scratched the stubble on his chin before speaking. "Well, one thing I have learned is that people experience and interact with the world around them in many different ways; there is no one 'right' way of thinking, learning, and behaving," said Earle. He picked up his magazine again.

"You're right. Thank you," she said, standing up, walking over to Earle, and kissing the top of his head. "And that gives me an idea."

Starting the very next day, Frances began spending many hours with Teodor, teaching him to read and write in English. The time spent helped him to overcome many of the social challenges he had faced all his life. He even developed the ability to participate in the conversations going on around him—as long as they involved Witez. His need for order and quiet remained, and Frances respected that.

New Year's Day, 1960 saw Calarabia Ranch hosting a grand party. Everyone who was involved in the Arabian show world was there. Tables were spread with food. A band played country western music. Dancers circled the wooden dance floor. Colored lights hung from the trees.

Teodor, now a handsome young man in his twenties, stayed with Witez, answering questions from the guests who wanted to meet the famous stallion.

One man, in particular, spent a great deal of time outside Witez's stall. Teodor thought nothing of it. Everyone loved to be with the horse.

As the sun set, Teodor fed Witez and the other stallions in the barn. He walked up to the main house, observing that most of the guests had departed. When he entered the living room, he noticed one man was still there, seated beside a woman and sitting across from the Hurlbutts.

Earle motioned him over. "Teodor, I want you to meet Mr. and Mrs. Betts, owners of the Circle 2 Ranch in Parker, Colorado."

The two strangers both stood offering him a smile and a handshake. Teodor recognized the man as the same who had spent so much time with Witez.

"You can call me Burr," said the man. "And this is my wife, Lucille."

Lucille extended her hand but quickly dropped it when Teodor neglected to take it. "Please call me, Lu," she said, offering the young man a warm smile. She was dressed in a red shirt-waist dress, perfect for the season. A string of pearls encircled her neck. Her hair was cut short with curls that framed her face.

Teodor noticed that Mr. Betts looked more like a citified businessman than a horse breeder. His wavy dark brown hair was graying at the temples. His clean-shaven face was angular and handsome. He wore a well-tailored, dark blue suit. A crisp white shirt adorned with a wide striped tie was beneath the jacket. But his pale eyes sparkled, and he had a ready smile. The man exuded confidence.

"It's nice to meet you," Teodor said softly.

Frances stepped up beside Teodor. "Teodor, there is something we want to tell you."

The tone of her voice was serious, and Teodor stiffened.

"We have agreed to send Witez to Colorado under a lease arrangement with Mr. and Mrs. Betts," she said.

Teodor jerked his head back. "What? Why would you do such a thing?"

Earle stepped up beside his wife. "I have known Burr Betts for many years. He has quite a reputation in the Arabian community. The Circle 2 Ranch is becoming a world-class breeding facility. From Colorado, Witez can expand his influence to more of the country."

"But he is doing just fine here," Teodor said.

"That's true, but his sons are doing a great job carrying on his line on the West Coast. The Betts can help improve the breed through the Midwest and East Coast from their more central location."

Teodor dropped his eyes and clenched his fists. "Teodor's horse," he whispered.

Burr Betts placed a hand on Teodor's shoulder. The young man stepped back. Betts lowered his hand without offense. "Teodor, Lu, and I would like you to come with Witez. We're sure you'll love Colorado and the beautiful Circle 2 Ranch."

"And we know Witez would not be happy without you," added Lu.

Chapter 38

Parker Colorado, 1960

Teodor didn't need to pack much. Other than suitable riding clothes, he didn't own much.

Frances gave him a warm jacket. "The Colorado winters can get cold," she told him as she handed him the newly purchased garment. She brushed a tear from her cheek.

Earle had a gift of his own. "Make sure they take good care of our boy," he said as he handed him a pair of thick gloves. "Now don't fall in love with Colorado, young man. We'll expect you back in four years when the lease is up."

Teodor merely nodded, his hands trembling, the muscles in his jaw twitching.

A week after the agreement was made, Burr Betts drove up to the barn, pulling a nice-looking white horse trailer with a Circle 2 logo painted on the side. Teodor watched him arrive, his hands twisting his cap, his lips pursed.

The truck stopped in front of him, and Burr Betts jumped out. "Mornin', Teodor," he said, smiling broadly. "Ready for a long drive?" The man looked more like a horseman today. He was now dressed in a plaid shirt and denim jeans. Cowboy boots covered his feet.

Teodor looked to the ground. "Yes, sir."

"Is Witez ready?"

"Yes, sir."

"Well, let's be on our way. The day isn't getting any longer."

Francis hustled out of the house with a basket of sandwiches, fruit, and cookies. To Burr she said, "Give our love to Lu when you get home." To Teodor all she could do was wipe away a tear and whisper, "I'll miss you."

Earle Hurlbutt came out of the barn leading Witez. "Here he is, Betts. I know you'll take good care of him. But remember, I want him bred to only the finest mares."

The drive to Colorado was a long one with overnight stops in Tucson and Albuquerque. The trip was made even longer due to the lack of conversation. Burr Betts, a naturally gregarious sort, had been warned about Teodor's peculiar nature, but he didn't realize just how peculiar until he spent three days alone with him in the cab of a pickup.

For Teodor's part, he was struggling to keep his emotions intact. When Betts turned up the radio for some entertainment, Teodor closed his eyes and pressed his hands over his ears. Noticing this reaction, Betts immediately turned the radio off. For mile after mile, they drove in silence. The hum of the tires on the asphalt was the only sound, but it was music to Teodor's ears.

The trip across the southwest desert went smoothly. On the third day, however, as they were crossing Raton pass at the New Mexico/Colorado border, they drove right into a blizzard. The snow was coming down fast and the wind blew it sideways, making it nearly impossible to see the road. Burr slowed down and struggled to keep the truck and trailer on the road. Teodor glanced over and noticed Burr's white knuckles as he gripped the steering wheel. The man's teeth were clenched, and the muscles of his jaw twitched as he peered through the windshield. The wipers had a hard time moving fast enough to keep the glass cleared.

"Should we stop?" Teodor said.

"No place on this narrow road. I'll just creep along."

For more than an hour, they worked their way up and over Raton Pass on the winding, slick roads, finally arriving in Trinidad. Burr pulled off the road and drove into town, parking along the brick-paved road in front of a local café. "I need a break," he said. "Hungry?"

"Starving," said Teodor as he wiped the perspiration off his forehead. "You did a good job driving."

Burr glanced over at the quiet young man. "Thanks," he said with a smile.

The Betts ranch was located just a few miles south of the tiny town of Parker, Colorado. The little town had a cute main street, appropriately named "Mainstreet," a post office, a feed store, a popular restaurant, and a school, but not much else.

The Circle 2 Ranch was accessed from the rural road called Hilltop, and the ranch was spread out over two thousand acres at the top of that hill from which the road got its name. The main house was a very large, rambling, single-story structure. Stone and dark timbers covered the exterior. The views from the house and just about everywhere else on the ranch took one's breath away, especially as the sun made its final descent of the day. To the south stood the majestic and proud 14,000-foot mountain called Pikes Peak, named after explorer Zebulon Pike. Straight out to the west was the wide and formidable mountain named Mount Evans after the territorial Governor by that name.

It was nearing the time for one of those beautiful sunsets when the truck and trailer pulled off Hilltop Road and into the ranch on a single-lane gravel drive. Betts drove past the main house and the large stable with an indoor arena, to a smaller barn off to one side. "This is the stallion barn where Witez will live. There is an apartment above the stalls that will be for you," Betts said as he pulled on the parking brake and turned off the engine. "Let's take care of Witez then head to the house for some of Lu's great cooking."

Witez was bedded down in a large box stall. There were five other stallions in the barn and each snorted and whinnied a greeting to Witez as he walked by. For his part, Witez merely lifted his head and tail and paraded right past. He was the chieftain, and he wanted everyone to know it.

Teodor ran his bag up the stairs and placed it on the foot of the bed in his new room. He paused just long enough to look around. It was a small but clean and pleasant apartment with a window that looked out at Pikes Peak. There was a small closet with more than enough room for his clothing. The private bathroom held a sink, toilet, and small shower. Everything met his needs perfectly.

Dinner in the Betts' large home was delicious. After the harrowing drive over the mountain pass, Burr Betts had quite a story to tell. Around the table sat Mr. Betts, Mrs. Betts, their son and only child, Burr Junior, who preferred to be called "Bob," and his pregnant wife, Mona. Bob looked very much like his mother. His wife was tall and beautiful with brown hair and eyes. She wore her pregnancy like a princess.

"Teodor, I'm eager to see you ride Witez," Mona said between mouthfuls of steaming hot shepherd's pie. "From what I hear, you two have been through quite a lot together."

Teodor looked down at his plate and straightened his napkin on his lap.

"Such experiences can't help but create a strong bond between man and horse," added Lu.

"Few people ever develop such a bond with their horse," said Mona. "We are often too busy with other things." She glanced over at her husband who didn't seem to be paying attention to the conversation.

Mona cleared her throat. "Well, be that as it may, I am the trainer here at the Circle 2. But, as you can see, I'm expecting a child soon. I'm going to need your help, not just with Witez but with the other horses as well."

Bob looked over at his father. "How are the plans coming for the Security Life building?"

Burr finished chewing, swallowed, and took a drink of water. "It is going to be fabulous. We are just securing the property on 16th street in downtown Denver. Then we'll finalize the plans and start with the permits."

"Are you still thinking of building a thirty-story skyscraper?" Bob asked.

Burr nodded, another bite of shepherd's pie filling his mouth.

Bob frowned. "Don't you think that is a bit excessive? Can Security Life and Accident Insurance Company afford such an extravagant building?"

Burr swallowed. "We already have several businesses who have committed to rent space."

Bob shook his head. "I don't like stretching our resources so far. You already spend a small fortune on those horses of yours. I hear you bought more mares from the man you leased this new horse from. Was that necessary?"

"It was necessary if we want a world-class Arabian breeding program," said Burr, firmly clutching his knife in his right hand and his fork in the other. "Besides, aren't you the one who just came home with an Elva Mark 5 racecar? I don't even want to know how much that cost."

"I needed it if I'm going to become a world-class driver."

Burr took another bite of the pie, chewed it briefly, and went on. "And I need Witez and the mares to become a world-class Arabian horse breeder."

"I guess that is another area where we disagree. I don't understand why you couldn't just enjoy yourself with the Round Up Riders of the Rockies on your Appaloosa, Mike, like you used to."

"You're right," Burr snapped. "You don't understand me, and I don't understand you."

Mona reached over and placed a hand on Bob's arm. He jerked away.

A queasy feeling spread through Teodor's gut.

Lu cleared her throat. "Pie, anyone?

Chapter 39

Circle 2 Ranch 1960-1964

Teodor settled into a comfortable routine at the ranch. He learned all that was expected of him in caring for the stallions. Feeding time was at exactly seven in the morning, twelve noon, and five in the evening, with a night check at nine. Stalls and runs were cleaned while the horses were on turnout in the paddocks.

The arrival of Mona's baby, a little girl she named Lisa, meant Teodor and the other ranch hands had even more work to do. Mona, being the head horse trainer, left specific instructions with Teodor about the training of each horse. Witez was Teodor's, but the other horses needed to be prepared for sale. The foals and yearlings required training in halter work and ground manners. Saddles and bridles were introduced to the two-year-olds. It was all very orderly, and Teodor thrived in just such an environment.

The stallions, all being old enough to ride, were exercised in the covered arena during the winter months and in the outdoor arena the rest of the year. Teodor always saved Witez for last. He loved taking the afternoons between feedings to ride Witez all around the ranch. He stopped at the top of each hill to gaze at the rugged peaks to the west, a view he never tired of.

The summer typically brought late afternoon thunderstorms. Teodor sat on Witez's back watching the dark clouds move toward them from the west. Gray streaks of rain fell like curtains across the foothills and moved their way toward Cherry Creek and the Circle 2. When the first shaft of lightning burst from the thunderheads, Teodor galloped Witez back to the stable. He had been warned about the dangers of being outside in a lightning storm. It wasn't uncommon to find the carcass of one of their head of cattle the morning after such a storm. Teodor was not going to let Witez fall victim to a lightning strike.

Burr Betts was busy with his business and the plans for his new skyscraper, as well as many community responsibilities. The groundbreaking for the new Security Life building was held on June 30, 1962 with an extravagant ceremony on 16th Street in Denver. The building was to be thirty stories high with the word, *Security*, proudly displayed across the top. Though invited to attend, Teodor chose to stay at the ranch with the horses. Large gatherings were difficult for him.

As it was, the ranch increasingly became the center of numerous social gatherings. Burr and Lu started sponsoring and hosting the annual spring Arabian show. Classes in English, Western, and even driving, were offered. Arabian horse owners and competitors from all over the state, and beyond, came with their horses while sleeping in campers or tents. Teodor kept himself busy and fairly hidden in the stallion barn. But Witez was the object of much attention, and many people wanted to see him to find out for themselves just what all the fuss was about regarding this foreign-born stallion. So, for several days each April, Teodor found himself showing Witez to visitor after visitor.

On October 7, 1963, another grand social event was held. The Betts organized a charity fundraiser they titled "Furs and Horses." The beautiful Arabians marched down the runway as their handlers modeled the latest in fashions from the fur industry. The tall and beautiful Mona was pictured in *The Denver Post* wearing a sable jacket over an elegant evening gown as she led her gray Arabian named Bakker in front of the admiring audience.

With the Circle 2 Ranch and the Betts family so involved in the social events of Denver, Teodor was pushed to the limits of his ability to function. He got quieter as the noise and attention around him increased. Witez, on the other hand, blossomed. It was as though the stallion felt he deserved the spotlight.

But even with all the glam and glitter, things were not going smoothly at the ranch for Witez. Teodor chanced to be in the main house one winter day in 1964 and overheard a heated conversation. Burr was on the phone, and from what he was saying, Teodor realized he was talking to the Hurlbutts in California.

"What do you mean you don't like the mares Witez is covering? I don't remember ever saying you got to choose which mares I got to breed Witez to. I'm leasing the horse. That means I am in charge of making those decisions."

Teodor peeked around the doorframe into the office. Betts was standing behind his desk, still tethered to his phone as he listened to the response, his face getting redder and redder by the second.

"Well, if that's the way you feel, perhaps we need to end this relationship. I will make arrangements to send the horse back." Betts slammed down the phone. He looked up and noticed Teodor standing by the door. "It looks like you are going back to California."

Chapter 40

Calarabia, 1965

While his time in Colorado had been a learning experience for him, especially under the tutelage of Mona, Teodor was happy to be back with the Hurlbutts in California. The ranch was peaceful and orderly. The Hurlbutts were a calm and quiet couple. Even their German Shepherd had aged gracefully and welcomed Teodor home with a single rub of his head against the young man's leg.

Witez seemed happy to be home as well. Even though his body was aging, he still had plenty of energy to gallop around his familiar pasture like a young colt. He whinnied at the other horses as if to announce that the Chieftain was back.

Several new fillies and colts pranced across the fields at their mothers' sides. The Hurlbutts introduced Teodor to each one, pride in their eyes. "This is Witez's grandson. This is Witez's granddaughter."

Teodor tickled each soft little muzzle and rubbed each fuzzy croup. Then he laughed as they lifted their fur-covered tails and pranced away. He threw his arms to the side and turned in a slow circle, breathing in the fresh air flowing down the mountainsides.

Earle Hurlbutt decided to retire Witez from stud, convinced his sons and daughters could carry on the legacy the stallion had brought from Poland to America. This meant that Teodor had Witez all to himself. Though the horse still seemed strong and healthy, majestic even, Teodor knew he needed to slow down. Their rides were shorter, the pace slower.

As he rode Witez up the foothills, he heard in his mind the tune and words to a lullaby that his mother always sang to him at bedtime. He had never joined in with her singing. In fact, he hadn't even thought of the little tune for years. Suddenly the words to the song left his mouth and floated up into the soft blue sky.

> Lie my little angel, lie and sleep,
> mum is rocking her baby,
> sleep sweet little one,
> mum is rocking her baby.

With the gentle rocking motion of the horse's walk, Teodor knew with certainty that he and Witez were home.

While Witez rolled in the grass and slept in the warm California sun, Teodor and the Hurlbutts enjoyed keeping track of the success of Witez's progeny. Witezar, a stallion whom the Hurlbutts bred at the Calarabia ranch, became the winner of the most points in the history of the American Horse Shows Association Horse of the Year Award. Son after son, and daughter after daughter took home the ribbons and championships at shows large and small. Some were making their mark on the racetrack. Others in the hunter-jumper ring. And still others showed their skill as carriage horses. The versatile horses displayed their stamina in endurance rides, trotting for a hundred miles, or danced around the dressage arena. Nothing could stop the legacy Witez brought to America.

One evening, as the fire crackled in the fireplace and the German Shepherd snored on the rug at Teodor's feet, Frances looked up from the bookwork she was struggling over. "Teodor," she said before taking a breath and brushing her curls back from her face.

Teodor looked at her mouth but avoided her eyes. He rubbed his hands on his pants and said, "Yes?"

"Do you remember the research I did before you left for Colorado?"

"Autism?"

"Yes. That's it."

"My mother was not cold and detached."

"I know. That didn't sound right to me, either."

Knowing she had his attention, she forged on. "I have read a new study that was just published in 1964 by a man named Bernard Rimland. He disputes the 'refrigerator mother' theory. Instead, he sees a neurological factor in autism. The neurons interact with one another in the brain. They tend to respond differently in different people."

"So, you think my brain doesn't work?" asked Teodor, his hands rubbing on his pant legs faster and faster.

"Oh, Teodor, that's not what I'm saying at all," Frances insisted. Watching his hands rubbing his legs, she added, "Each of us works a little differently. I'm just trying to help you understand why you struggle to control your behaviors and reactions to new situations."

She got up from her chair and kneeled in front of him. "You are a remarkable young man. I have seen you make so much progress in your ability to interact with people. And your ability to work with horses is the envy of everyone. All of that is probably because of Witez."

Teodor looked over her head at the flickering flames. A smile spread across his face as he thought of Witez.

On April 1, 1965, the Hurlbutts held a grand party for Witez's twenty-seventh birthday. Fans from all around the Arabian world came to pay their respects. Balloons and streamers decorated the fence line at the edge of the property and up the drive to the house. Tables laden with food sat on the front lawn. A table just for desserts held carrot cakes, oatmeal cookies, and apple pies in honor of Witez's favorite treats.

All the guests greeted Witez with rubs and hugs, and Witez loved it. At twenty-seven, he still looked fabulous. True, his muscles were less defined, and specks of gray dotted his brown coat while a few white hairs grew from his mane. But his eyes still sparkled with intelligence, and his ears pricked forward and back, catching every soothing compliment and every whispered tribute.

The party went long into the night, and Teodor found himself wishing it would end so the quiet could return to the ranch. He hid himself away in Witez's stall and brushed the stallion's mane again and again. He stayed with the horse until he heard the last of the cars crunching on the gravel as they moved down the drive and out onto the road. Only then did he leave the stallion barn and return to the house.

Frances and Earle were still up, putting food away. Teodor gathered some dishes to help.

"Such a fun party," gushed Frances. "Did you enjoy yourself, Teodor?"

Teodor nodded.

Frances turned to face him. "I know large groups and lots of noise are hard for you, but I appreciate your help showing Witez to our guests. He really is Teodor's horse, and everyone knows it."

Teodor lowered his chin and smiled.

Chapter 41

Two months later, on June 9, Teodor awakened slowly and rubbed his eyes. Suddenly, he noticed that the sun was too high and the room too bright. He sat up with a start and threw back the covers. Shocked that he had overslept—something he never did—he dashed down the stairs, two at a time. He pulled open the kitchen door. The scent of last night's rain blew in. He stepped through the door and jumped off the porch.

He didn't know how he knew it, but a chill of dreadful certainty rippled through him. Something was wrong.

Impatient for breakfast, the other stallions stood at the fences of their paddocks looking at him. They whinnied their displeasure at being forced to wait for their grain. But no bay head with a bright white star awaited his arrival. No deep, throaty whinny called out to him. Witez was not there.

Teodor started running. Climbing the fence to Witez's paddock, he swung both legs over the top rail and landed on the far side with both feet. He looked from side to side, scanning the waving spring grasses. Then he heard the Hurlbutts' German Shepherd howl. Teodor ran toward the sound, his long legs covering the distance across the paddock in a few dozen strides.

Teodor skidded to a stop when he saw the bay body stretched on its side. No movement lifted his barrel in a rhythmic up and down pattern. No tail swatted at the flies buzzing around it. No head lifted to greet him.

The dog walked slowly over to the young man and sat beside him. His howling stopped. He had no more to say.

The pain cut through Teodor's heart like a scythe. He dropped to his knees beside Witez. A guttural groan rose from deep inside, and he threw his body over the horse. Tears streamed down his cheeks as he pleaded with Witez.

"Don't leave me, Witez," he sobbed. "I can't make it without you." Throwing his head back and looking to the sky he wailed. "No-o-o-o-o."

The German Shepherd curled up beside him.

A solemn graveside service was held that afternoon. Teodor and Earle placed a stone at the head of the mound of dirt that covered Witez in his resting place. Later, the stone would be replaced by a beautiful marble plaque. Both Frances and Earle shared the love they felt for the brave stallion who had withstood the evils of war and come to America to share his great talents.

Teodor said nothing as he looked down at Witez's grave. Frances handed Teodor a Bible. A fringed bookmark stuck out the top. He mumbled a "Thank you" then turned and retreated to his room in the ranch house.

Teodor pulled the spread off the bed and wrapped it around himself until it was so tight that he couldn't move. He dropped onto the bed in his cocoon. He closed his eyes, pressed his lips into a straight line, and let himself fall into the darkness. He seemed to descend forever, spiraling down and down toward a bottomless pit. He moaned and rolled from side to side. That is where he stayed throughout the sleepless night.

When the first sign of silver light whispered that the sun would soon make its appearance for a new day, he opened one eye. He watched the silver light become golden and the gray sky become blue. He looked to the table beside his bed and noticed the Bible laying there where he had tossed it. He wiggled his arms loose from the wrap that still enveloped him and reached for the book. Gently, he opened it to the page that had been marked. He noticed one verse had been highlighted with blue ink: Joshua 1:9. He read the verse.

Be strong and of a good courage; be not afraid, neither be thou dismayed:
for the Lord thy God is with thee whithersoever thou goest.

Teodor sat up and swung his legs off the side of the bed. He clasped the Bible to his chest. Closing his eyes, he started rocking forward and back, forward and back. A whimper escaped his lips. Memories of his home in Hostau ran through his mind: the first day he met Witez, and because of that meeting, the first words he spoke: Teodor's horse . . . the hours of riding through the forest on the stallion's strong back, feeling the power beneath him and hearing the rhythmic pounding of his hooves . . . the fear he felt as the shells fell close to the stables, sending blasts vibrating through his body . . . the escape across the border . . . the treacherous ocean crossing.

He had been courageous then, but this was too much. Then, he had been brave . . . for Witez. No. That wasn't it at all. Witez had been brave for him. Witez had carried him through everything.

He suddenly realized Witez had been sent to him for a grand and noble purpose.

But now Witez was gone.

He dropped the Bible and it fell to the floor at his feet. His hands started shaking as he continued to rock—forward and back, forward and back. The all-consuming pain and fear forced all other emotions from him. There was no room for rational thoughts. No decisions or plans could possibly be made for a future he could not picture.

Sometime later, Teodor heard a soft tap at his door. He turned away and closed his eyes. His hands continued to shake; his body still rocked.

The hinges squeaked as the door was pushed open.

"Teodor," Hurlbutt said, his voice soft and uncertain. "Teodor, I need your help."

Teodor felt a growl rumble in the back of his throat.

"Teodor," Hurlbutt repeated, this time with more conviction. "I have something very important that I need help with."

Teodor opened his eyes. He turned toward Hurlbutt. Taking a deep breath and letting it out with a huff, he forced himself to stand.

"Follow me, Teodor," Hurlbutt said.

With Teodor shuffling a few paces behind, Hurlbutt walked down the hall to the living room. He turned and looked back at Teodor with a smile on his face and a tear in his eye. Brushing the tear aside, he reached for the doorknob. "Come outside with me."

Hurlbutt stepped out onto the long front porch. Frances was standing in the front yard, holding the lead rope attached to the halter of a beautiful bay yearling colt. The horse had Witez's white star on his forehead and the same white socks on each pastern. His black mane and tail fluttered in the gentle morning breeze.

Extending her hand, Frances offered the end of the lead rope to Teodor.

Hurlbutt gave the young man a gentle push toward the yearling. He cleared his throat and choked out the words:

"Teodor's horse."

Author's Note:

As implied in the preamble, this story is based on the life of the famous Polish Arabian Stallion Witez II. Most of the events in the horse's life are as accurate as I was able to determine based upon the resources available. The names of most of the people in Witez's life, including the American and German officers, and the Americans who later owned or leased him, are accurate. The places where he lived are also correct. However, this is historical fiction. That means I took liberties with the dialogue and a few experiences. While writing the dialogue, I did my best to portray the characters' personalities as I understand them to be.

Teodor and his mother, Agata, are fictional characters. The German Army really did use both prisoners of war and local villagers to act as grooms for the large number of horses at the Hostau Stud. Therefore, it was fitting that Teodor could work as a groom at the Stud. Grooms also traveled with the horses as they crossed the Atlantic and came to America.

Very little was understood about autism during the years covered in this book. Indeed, we still have much to learn. However, as a result of my work with the Professional Association of Therapeutic Horsemanship, PATH International, I learned that horses have an amazing power to help children and adults who struggle with autism. I tried to illustrate the remarkable impact horses have through the relationship between Witez and Teodor. If you know a child or adult with autism, consider getting them involved with horse therapy. Go to pathintl.org to find a therapy center near you.

I hope you enjoyed reading "The Stallion and His Peculiar Boy" as much as I did researching and writing it.

Please post a review on Amazon, Barnes and Noble, or Goodreads.

Sign up for my newsletter to receive notification regarding new releases and other book news. Email me at: mjevansbtm@gmail.com to request the newsletter. Put "Special Gift" in the subject line and receive a free copy of the short story "The Christmas Colt."

M.J. Evans

M.J. Evans is the award-winning, best-selling author of twenty-two books, most of which are centered around horses or horse-fantasy creatures. As a life-long equestrian, she loves combining her love of horses with her passion for writing.

Born and raised in Oregon and a graduate of Oregon State University, she is a former teacher of junior high and high school students. She now lives in Colorado with her husband Tom, a standard poodle, and two horses. Her proudest accomplishment is raising five children without ever having to visit them in prison! Those same wonderful children have given her twelve incredible grandchildren and lots of names to use in her books.

Please visit her website to see all her books: www.dancinghorsepress.com

Follow her on:

Amazon Author page:
https://www.amazon.com/M.-J.-Evans/e/B004GMS014

Facebook – margi.evans.98

Instagram - mjevansbooks

Twitter - @mjevansauthor

Pinterest - MJEvansFantasyNovelist/

Goodreads - author/show/4496514.M_J_Evans

Acknowledgments

I am so grateful for the help of my Editor, Denny Dressman, former Senior Editor for The *Rocky Mountain News* and the author of fifteen non-fiction books, nine of which are about sports figures. He went through every chapter to make sure I was doing a good job!

I am thankful to Tracy Guy Urrutia. Tracy is the manager of the Parker, Colorado Dover Saddlery store. But more importantly, she is the mother of an autistic son. She was kind enough to read my manuscript and verify that Teodor's behaviors were consistent with someone on the Autism Spectrum.

I live just outside Parker, Colorado. So, I was thrilled to learn that Witez actually spent four years of his life here. I am grateful for Cade Benson of Elizabeth, Colorado, who was married to Mona Betts until she passed away. He was so generous with his time answering my questions.

Brian Trembath at the Western History Department of the Denver Public Library helped me find information about the Betts family.

Liz Syverson spent much time sharing what she knew about the Betts family as well.

Bibliography

Books:

Felton, Mark, *Ghost Riders: When US and German Soldiers Fought Together to Save the World's Most Beautiful Horses in the Last Days of World War II* (Da Capo Press, 2018)

Isaacson, Rupert, *The Horse Boy, A Memoir of Healing* (Little, Brown and Company, 2009)

Letts, Elizabeth, *The Perfect Horse: The Daring U.S. Mission to Rescue the Priceless Stallions Kidnapped by the Nazis* (Ballantine Books, 2016)

Smith, Linell, *And Miles to Go – The Biography of a Great Arabian Horse, Witez II* (Little, Brown and Company, 1967)

Additional Titles by M.J. Evans

The Sand Pounder – Love and Drama on Horseback in WWII
First Place: Maincrest Media Awards
First Place: Royal Dragonfly book Awards
First Place: Pinnacle Book Awards
Finalist: Chanticleer Intl. Book Awards
Finalist: The Wishing Shelf Book Awards (UK)
Finalist: Independent Press Book Awards

PINTO! Based Upon the True Story of the Longest Horseback Ride in History
First Place: Book Excellence Awards
First Place: Chanticleer Intl. Book Awards
First Place: Purple Dragonfly Awards
Plus seven other literary awards: Eric Hoffer Award, Readers' Favorite Award, American Fiction Award and more.

In the Heart of a Mustang
First Place: Literary Classics Awards
First Place: Equus Film Festival
Second Place: Nautilus Awards
Second Place: Readers' Favorite Awards

The Mist Trilogy-Behind the Mist,
Mists of Darkness, The Rising Mist
Gold medal from the Mom's Choice Award
First Place: Equus Film Festival

North Mystic
First Place: Purple Dragonfly Awards

The Centaur Chronicles–
The Stone of Mercy, The Stone of Courage,
The Stone of Integrity, The Stone of Wisdom
Gold, Silver and Bronze Medals: Feathered
Quill Book Awards
Silver Medal: Readers' Favorite Awards
Finalist: Book Excellence Award
First Place: Equus Film Festival
Purple Dragonfly Award
New Apple ebook Award

PERCY –
The Racehorse Who Didn't Like to Run
First Place: Purple Dragonfly Award
Gold Medal: Literary Classics Book Awards
Silver Medal: Feathered Quill Awards

Mr. Figgletoes' Toy Emporium
First Place: Feathered Quill Book Award
First Place: TopShelf Book Awards
Finalist: Book Excellence Award
Finalist: Wishing Shelf Book Award (UK)
Winner: Purple Dragonfly Award

*The Skullington Family Series: Boney Fingers,
Bone Appetit, School is a Grave Mistake, and
Skeletons in the Closet*
Readers' Favorite Five Star Award
Mom's Choice Gold Medal

Equestrian Trail Guidebooks:
*Riding Colorado-
Day Trips from Denver with Your Horse
Riding Colorado II-
Day Trips from Denver with Your Horse
Riding Colorado III-
Day and Overnight Trips with Your Horse
Riding Colorado and Beyond-
Overnight Trips In and Around Colorado*

All fiction titles are available on the Website:
www.dancinghorsepress.com   and   wherever
books are sold.

DANCING HORSE PRESS